brave

Svetlana Chmakova

SVETLANA CHMAKOVA

Coloring assistant: Melissa McCommon

Lettering: JuYoun Lee

1290 Avenue of the Americas
New York, NY 10104

Visit us at yenpress.com
facebook.com/yenpress
twitter.com/yenpress
yenpress.tumblr.com
instagram.com/yenpress

First JY Edition: May 2017

JY is an imprint of Yen Press, LLC.
The JY name and logo are trademarks of Yen Press, LLC.

The publisher is not responsible for websites (or their content) that are not owned by the publisher.

Library of Congress Control Number: 2017934376

Hardcover ISBN: 978-0-316-36317-4
Paperback ISBN: 978-0-316-36318-1

10 9 8

LSC-C

Printed in the United States of America

Table of Contents

CHAPTER 1

MY NAME IS JENSEN. JENSEN GRAHAM.
I MAY BE JUST A REGULAR KID AT REGULAR BERRYBROOK MIDDLE SCHOOL...
...BUT I AM GOING TO SAVE THE WORLD.

PEOPLE ARE OBLIVIOUS...
...BUT SO MANY DANGERS LURK!!
SUNSPOTS ARE THE BIG ONE...I'M STILL FIGURING THAT ONE OUT...BUT SAY...

...IF THERE'S AN EARTHQUAKE?
I KNOW **EXACTLY** WHAT TO DO.
AND FOR A TORNADO TOO!

ZOMBIE diaries
...AND...OH! IF IT'S A ZOMBIE APOCALYPSE?

I HAVE A LIST OF **WARNING SIGNS** IN MY POCKET.
ZOMBIE SURVIVAL GUIDE
(IN THE SAME POCKET, I ALSO HAVE A PROTEIN BAR AND A GAME BOY. IN CASE I HAVE TO BARRICADE MYSELF IN THE MAINTENANCE ROOM...)

...THERE ARE MANY ZOMBIE WARNING SIGNS IN MY MATH CLASS...
URGH
I BETTER BE CAREFUL.

...OF COURSE, IT COULD JUST BE THAT THIS IS MATH...

...WITH MR. KRISTOFFER, THE MOST BORING AND EVIL MATH TEACHER IN THE UNIVERSE.
PAY ATTENTION, CLASS, OR IT'S EXTRA HOMEWORK AGAIN FOR EVERYONE!

I HAAAAATE MATH.
BUT MOM SAID I'LL NEED IT FOR WHAT I WANT TO BE—

AN ASTRONAUT AT NASA!

I CAN'T WAIT TO BE A REAL ASTRONAUT.
I'M GOING TO BEAT THE LONGEST SPACE WALK RECORD...
WHEE!
...AND WHEN I GO TO MARS, I'M GONNA DISCOVER AN ANCIENT CIVILIZATION.
earth
DUST
DUST
alien statue
...JENSEN.
JENSEN...?
JENSEN!!
...FOR THE LAST TIME, WHAT IS THE CORRECT ANSWER TO THIS PROBLEM?

42÷5/8=?

UH...
UM...

IS...IT...
...67?
68!
...81?
NO, IT MOST CERTAINLY IS NOT!

NO.
!
NO...
NOOOO
THAT'S IT!! EXTRA HOMEWORK FOR EVERYONE!! TWENTY PROBLEMS BY TOMORROW!!

GRRR
THANKS A LOT!
...
WTH, JENSEN?
AGAIN?
I WISH THE ZOMBIE SURVIVAL GUIDE COVERED SITUATIONS LIKE THIS...

RRRING
GRUMBLE
stupid jensen.
GLARE
...
...

IT'S OKAY. NEXT CLASS WILL BE BETTER.
IT'S ENGLISH! I REALLY LIKE THE TEACHER, MISS LEE...

...AND I HAVE A FRIEND THERE, PENELOPE TORRES..
WE'RE IN THE ART CLUB TOGETHER.
I JUST NEED TO GET THERE WITHOUT—

!
HEY, FATSO.

WHEN ARE YOU GONNA LEARN FRACTIONS, PEA BRAIN?
IF WE HAVE TO DO **ANY MORE** HOMEWORK BECAUSE OF YOU, I'M GONNA MAKE YOU REGRET IT. GOT THAT?

I-I...
I'M SORRY...?
NOT *YET*, YOU ARE
SNAP SNAP
HEY, WHAT'S GOING ON HERE?
...!

JENNY!!
FOSTER?
YANIC?
IS THERE A PROBLEM?

UH...NO...
WE GOTTA GET TO CLASS.
LATER!
LATER, JENSEN.
BUT HOPEFULLY NEVER!

I DIDN'T GET ANY GOOD PICTURES.
IT'S OKAY. WE'LL GET THOSE TROLLS NEXT TIME.
H-HI, GUYS!
HMPF
...THIS IS JENNY, AKILAH, AND FELIPE.
THEY RUN THE SCHOOL NEWSPAPER AND A POPULAR VLOG. **NO ONE** WANTS TO MESS WITH THEM.

JUST DROPPING OFF THIS ARTICLE ON MY WAY TO DISCOVER THE SECRETS OF ANCIENT MAYAN TEMPLES.

JENSEN, THIS IS FRONT-PAGE MATERIAL!! SUNSPOTS ARE REALLY THIS DANGEROUS?!! I MUST PRINT THIS IMMEDIATELY!!

WATCH WHERE YOU'RE GOING, YOU FAT WEIRDO!
...AS I SAID, DANGER LURKS EVERYWHERE.

THOSE NATURAL DISASTERS I MENTIONED BEFORE?
SLINK SLINK
MIDDLE SCHOOL IS IN THE TOP TEN.
SLINK SLINK
EACH DAY IS LIKE RUNNING THE GAUNTLET.

I THINK OF IT LIKE A VIDEO GAME.
I JUST HAVE TO GET THROUGH EACH DAY...

START!
...WITHOUT GETTING EATEN BY THE GAME MONSTERS...
MORE WORK!
GRRR
YOU SUCK!
HSSS
CHOMP
CHOMP
...TO WIN THE PRIZE AT THE END OF THE LEVEL...

THE ART CLUB
...WHERE I CAN JUST SIT, DRAW, AND NO ONE EVER BOTHERS ME.
I JUST HAVE TO MAKE IT TO THE END OF THE DAY...
ENGLIS
its ≠ it's
their ≠ they're
your ≠ you're
...OKAY, GUYS, SETTLE DOWN! THIS IS ENGLISH, NOT A TRIP TO THE ZOO!
I'M GOING TO FINISH TAKING ATTENDANCE NOW.

...PENELOPE TORRES?
HERE!
THAT'S HER! MY FRIEND FROM ART CLUB.

I THINK...SHE'S *DRAWING* SOMETHING.

STRETCH

JENSEN GRAHAM?
....!
UH, HERE!

JORGE RUIZ?
HERE.
...I'M GONNA SKETCH TOO.

I'VE BEEN ON A BIG SPACESHIP KICK LATELY...
NASA SAYS THEY NEED NEW SHIP DESIGNS, SO I—

MISS TORRES.
MR. GRAHAM.
PUT THOSE SKETCHES AWAY AND PAY ATTENTION PLEASE.

WE'RE STARTING ON GROUP PRESENTATIONS TODAY.

EVERYONE, PICK YOUR GROUPS NOW!
NO MORE THAN THREE PEOPLE PER GROUP AND NO FEWER THAN TWO, FOR OBVIOUS REASONS.

GROUP OF TWO?
THAT'S ME AND PENELOPE! I'M GONNA ASK...

HEY, PENELOPE! WANNA BE IN OUR GROUP?
!!
YEAH, OKAY!

...

HEY, MATT! YOU, ME— GROUP?
OKAY.
MELISSA, YOU'RE IN MINE!
UH.
UM.

THERE'S... NO ONE ELSE I CAN ASK.

DO YOU HAVE A GROUP, JENSEN?

UH... N-NO...
OKAY, WHO'S GOT ROOM FOR JENSEN?

UH... NOT US!
WE'VE ALREADY GOT THREE.
US TOO.
I COULD... JUST BE MY OWN GROUP.

ALL RIGHT, I NEED A VOLUNTEER TO LEAVE THEIR GROUP TO BE JENSEN'S PARTNER!
I'LL DO IT, MISS LEE.

...

GREAT! THANK YOU, JORGE!
NOW, EACH GROUP WILL PICK A PRESENTATION TOPIC WHILE I HAND OUT THE GUIDELINES.

YAMMER
CHATTE
HA HA

BASEBALL.
H-HUH?

FOR THE TOPIC?
...O-OH!
Y-YEAH, OKAY.

...
...
...

LIBRARY
RRRRING

HELP, MRS. PRATT, I HAVE TO PRETEND I KNOW BASEBALL!
TAKA TAKA
OH? HMM. LET'S SEE...

HOW ABOUT *BASEBALL FOR IDIOTS*?
—OOF, WHAT AN UNFORTUNATE TITLE.

I DON'T CARE!!
IT'S **PERFECT!**
CAN I HAVE IT, PLEASE?!!

LIBRARY
YUS.
I **SO** GOT THIS.
*...AND **THAT** IS HOW I WILL SAVE THE WORLD...*
*...BY BEING PREPARED FOR **ANYTHING**.*

IF THERE ARE PROBLEMS, I WILL **SOLVE** THEM.
IF THERE ARE THINGS I DON'T KNOW, I WILL **LEARN** THEM.
IF THERE ARE OBSTACLES, I WILL—
...
...HIDE AND LET THE GAME MONSTERS PASS.
...AFTER ALL THAT STUFF IN MATH AND ENGLISH...
COMPUTER CLASS
...THE REST OF TODAY'S LEVEL IS ACTUALLY PRETTY EASY.

WE'RE MAKING MINI GAMES IN COMPUTER CLASS...

...PLAYING VERY BADLY IN MUSIC...
(BUT MR. HISAYA IS SO OLD, HE CAN BARELY HEAR THAT WE SOUND LIKE A TRAIN WRECK.)

...AND TRYING VERY, VERY HARD NOT TO FAIL SCIENCE.
—QUANTUM PHYSICS IS A FASCINATING FIELD WITH MANY APPLICATIONS...

...AND THEN...

TIC TOC TIC TOC

PRING

...IT'S FINALLY...

SKIDD

WHO'S READY TO DRRRRAW?!

...TIME FOR ART CLUB!!

JENSEN, HA-HA! WE *STILL* HAVEN'T GOTTEN RID OF YOU?

HEY, CAPTAIN SUNSPOTS.

HEY, GUYS! WHAT ARE YOU ALL DRAWING?

CAN I SEEEE?

ELVES RIDE HORSES! AND LIVE IN FORESTS!
SAYS *YOU*! *MINE* ARE BADASS BIKER ELVES.
...THEY DO LOOK LIKE ELVES...
OMG, YOU GUYS, STOP WHATEVER IT IS YOU ARE DOING!!!
PEPPI? WHA—

I HAVE THE BEST. NEWS.
JAIME AND I WERE JUST IN THE LIBRARY, AND—

WHAT, DID HE PROPOSE OR SOMETHING?
HA HA HA HA HA
...UGH, *NO*! STOPPIT, TESS!

YOU GUYS, WE WERE TALKING TO MRS. PRATT JUST NOW, AND SHE SAID...
...THAT THEY ARE GOING TO HAVE AN **ARTS FESTIVAL!**
RIGHT HERE AT OUR SCHOOL!!
WITH A COSTUME CONTEST, PRIZES, AND EVEN *AUTHOR* EVENTS!

AND GUESS WHO ONE OF THE AUTHORS IS—

J.Y. SMITH!!
my badly drawn life
by J.Y. Smith
VOLUME 5

SHUT UP!
I LOVE HIS BOOKS!
WHAAA!?
....!

I KNOW, RIGHT??
....?
AND ANOTHER GUEST IS INA CRUZ, THE MANGA ARTIST!!

SHE'S GONNA DO A DRAWING WORKSHOP!!

ARE YOU KIDDING ME RIGHT NOW?? I HAVE ALL OF INA'S BOOKS!
YES!
YES!
YESSS!
WHAT...WHAT IS THIS? ARE OUR BIRTHDAYS EARLY OR SOMETHING THIS YEAR?

MRS. PRATT SAID THEY NEED LOTS OF ART—THE LOGO, A POSTER, THANK-YOU CARDS FOR THE AUTHORS...
WHO WANTS TO HELP?

MEEEEEEE!!
ME TOO!
DIBS ON THE THANK-YOU CARDS!
...I'LL HELP!

...I...
...ACTUALLY...
...HAVE NO IDEA WHO ANY OF THOSE AUTHORS ARE...
...BUT I CAN FIND OUT...?

LIBRARY

...BY INA CRUZ AND J.Y. SMITH? HMMM.
TAKA TAKA
THOSE ARE POPULAR BOOKS.

LOOKS LIKE ALL THE COPIES ARE OUT...
DO YOU WANT ME TO PUT YOU ON THE WAITING LIST?

UUHHH...

...YES.

...
SCHOOL'S SO EMPTY ALREADY.
...NO ZOMBIE APOCALYPSE AGAIN TODAY, HUH...? ...YAY?

BLEAH RRRG GRAR
I'D LURE ALL THE ZOMBIES TO THE CAFETERIA...
THAT'S TOO BAD. I HAVE AN **AWESOME** PLAN FOR THAT.

RAWR ARGH WAH
...AND THEN PROP UP THE DOOR WITH A FOLDING TABLE!!

BRREEP!
AUGH!

...JUST A TEXT FROM MOM...
THANKS FOR THE HEART ATTACK, MOM!
I THOUGHT THERE WAS A ZOMBIE IN MY POCKET...

...WELL, A
ZOMBIE HAND...
OR MAYBE...

EXIT
...A ZOMBIE
FOOT—
HA HA HA HA
HUH?

IT'S THEM!
WHY ARE THEY
HERE SO LATE?

HEY...
IS THAT...?
HUH?

THEY SAW ME!!!
EXIT
HEY,
JENSEN!
COME
OVER
HERE!

JENSEN!!

CHAPTER 2

HUFF
HUFF

HEY, JENSEN! WAIT UUUP!

PANT
PANT
NOPE! NOPE, NOPE!
WHAT SHOULD I DO, WHAT SHOULD I DO?!

CAFETERIA
...!

...THE CAFETERIA!!
I...I CAN USE MY ZOMBIE PLAN!

TUG
TUG
TUG
TUG
...IT'S LOCKED?!

OH, JENSEEEN!

NO, NO, NO, NO!!

HUFF
HUFF
WHERE'D HE GO?
DOWN THE STAIRS?
...!

HUFF HUFF
THERE'S ONE...

... MORE...
...PLACE...
HUFF
GASP
NEWSPAPER OFFICE
...TO TRY...

J-JENNY? AKILAH?
I-IS ANYONE THERE?
BAM
BAM

CLICK
...JENSEN?

AND SO—!

SHUFF SHUFF
SHUFF
TAKA TAKA
HOW ABOUT THIS FOR THE...
TOO BLURRY.
I'M SAFE HERE.

THESE THREE ARE LIKE A COMIC BOOK JUSTICE POWER TEAM.

JENNY IS THE CAPTAIN...

...AND AKILAH THE RIGHT-HAND COMMANDER...

...WHILE FELIPE IS LIKE THE ROGUE PILOT WHO CRASH-LANDS A LOT BUT ALWAYS COMPLETES HIS MISSION.

THEY EVEN HAVE THEIR OWN HEADQUARTERS!!
WITH A COUCH!
A VIDEO CORNER!
A MISSION PLANNING TABLE!!
AWESOME WALL OF POSTERS AND MAPS!!

...WE GOOFED AROUND TOO MUCH AND DIDN'T GET OUR COMICS IN ON TIME...

DO YOU THINK JENNY WAS SERIOUS ABOUT CANCELING THE NEWSLETTER IF WE'RE LATE?

I-I GUESS WE'LL FIND OUT.

...SHE WAS SERIOUS.

THAT IS HOW WE FOUND OUT THAT ONE DOES **NOT** MESS WITH JENNY.

SO

OMG

CANCELED.

P.S. i hate you.

...Y-YEAH.
I'M REALLY HOPING SHE FORGOT...SO I CAN SHOW HER MY SUNSPOTS ARTICLE...

HEY, JENSEN!
....!
WILL YOU HELP US PUT THESE FLYERS UP AROUND THE SCHOOL?

...
GLANCE
GLANCE
...

...ARE YOU LOOKING FOR FOSTER AND YANIC?
....!

LOOKING? HA-HA, NO! NO.
JUST...JUST MAKING SURE THEY'RE NOT HERE.

THEY MUST BUG YOU A LOT, HUH?
...!
OH, UH...

...WELL, I MEAN, IT'S FOSTER AND YANIC. THEY BUG EVERYONE...
...SO...
...
...
POINT POINT

...JENSEN, WE COULD ACTUALLY USE YOUR HELP WITH A PROJECT OF OURS.

M-MY HELP?!
...THAT'S WHAT I SAID...
YES!!
WHATEVER YOU NEED!

GREAT. DROP BY AGAIN, UH—
TOMORROW? WHAT DO WE HAVE...?
TOMORROW'S SUPER BUSY. WE HAVE TO FINISH THE SURVEYS.
MAYBE NEXT WEEK THOUGH? FELIPE'S GOT A FREE DAY ON TUESDAY.
STAPLE STAPLE

THURSDAY!
STAPLE
STAPLE
UH, THURSDAY! I MEANT THURSDAY.

...FELIPE, NO, WHAT ARE YOU DOING?!
I SAID ONE FLYER EVERY TEN FEET...

...NOT TEN FLYERS IN ONE FOOT!
BUT PEOPLE WILL SEE THIS BETTER!

NO, NO, NO, THIS IS TOO MUCH!
...WAIT, I LIKE THIS!

NEWSPAPER
SUBMISSIONS CALL!!!
SUBMIT:
•articles!!
•photos!!
...YOU DO?
...!
YEAH! IT STANDS OUT!
SEE? FELIPE DID GOOD!
articles!
•photos!
•quizzes

...SUBMISSION CALL?!
...I CAN SUBMIT MY SUNSPOTS ARTICLE!!

THE NEXT DAY.

START!

MATH IS EVIL AGAIN, ARGH!
EVERYONE, HAND IN THOSE TWENTY PROBLEMS FROM YESTERDAY **NOW**!
GROAN
UGH
...
NOOO, I WANT TO WORK ON MY ARTICLE...

BLAH BLAH BLAH BLAH BLAH BLAH BLAH
BUT I HAVE TO GET THROUGH IT...

...SO THAT, WHEN I'M A NASA ASTRONAUT ON THE INTERNATIONAL SPACE STATION, ON MY WAY TO JUPITER...

...I JUST WANT TO SAY TO EVERYONE DOWN THERE ON EARTH— MR. KRISTOFFER IS EVIL, AND HE WAS TOTALLY WRONG ABOUT ME!

CAPTAIN JENSEN GRAHA

what! is that jensen?!

HEH-HEH-HEH.

JENSEN.

JENSEN!

I HATE HAVING GYM BEFORE LUNCH.
I GET ALL TIRED AND SWEATY...

...AND THE GAME MONSTERS NOTICE.
DASH
...EWWW, WHO'S THE STINK BOMB?
HA HA

I HAVE TO STAY VIGILANT.
GLANCE GLANCE
I HAVEN'T SEEN YANIC AND FOSTER TODAY YET...WONDER IF THEY'RE OUT SICK?

THAT'D BE GREAT. I COULD GET TO LUNCH WITHOUT ENGAGING LURK MODE.

HACK COUGH
BUT WAIT.
WHAT IF THEY'RE SICK AND IN SCHOOL?

...THAT'S HOW ZOMBIE EPIDEMICS START, THAT'S WHAT!
RAWR
BITE
AAAAA! what the-
IS THIS A NEW GAME?
HMMM.
YANIC AND FOSTER COULD INFECT THE WHOLE SCHOOL!!
BRAAINS... RAWR
RRING
CAFETERIA
...I'M SO GLAD I HAVE A ZOMBIE SURVIVAL PLAN.
I'LL BE ABLE TO SAVE ALL MY ART FRIENDS.

IT WOULD BE EASY, SINCE WE ALWAYS SIT TOGETHER AT LUNCH.
HEY, GUYS!
hi, jensen!

OH, LOOK, IT'S THE SUNSPOTS KID!
SAVED THE WORLD TODAY YET?
NOT YET! WORKING ON IT...
TESS AND I ALWAYS JOKE AROUND LIKE THIS. SHE'S REALLY FUNNY.

...OOOH, BOLOGNA SANDWICH TODAY!
SO...
RRUSTLE

PING
...LOOKS LIKE EVERY DESIGN TASK FOR THE ART FEST IS SPOKEN FOR, YAY!
THANKS FOR VOLUNTEERING, GUYS!

OH!
I WANNA HELP WITH THAT TOO!

WELL, THEN YOU SHOULD'VE RESPONDED TO THE GROUP CHAT, LIKE WE ASKED.
HUH?
WHAT CHAT?
THE GROUP CHAT FROM ***YESTERDAY NIGHT***, JENSEN.

YESTERDAY?
I DIDN'T...
...SEE ANY CHAT...
...UH-OH. DID I MISS SOMETHING AGAIN?

...U-UH.
TESS?
I DON'T SEE HIM ON THE LIST YOU MADE.
I don't think he ever got invited...

...

...OH.

JENSEN, I AM ***SO*** SORRY!!
IT'S... IT'S OKAY.
I'M DOING THE POSTER WITH TESS AND NINA. DO YOU WANT TO HELP US?

OH! N-NO, THAT'S OKAY.
...

...ANYWAY!
DID YOU GUYS SEE THAT NEW TRAILER FOR *STAR WARS*?
OH! IS IT OUT?
...THIS IS SO AWKWARD.

RRRING

ENGLISH
...BUT, YAY, ENGLISH IS NEXT! I'M **SO** GLAD I HAVE A PARTNER FOR THAT PRESENTATION.

BASEBALL.
...EVEN IF IT'S THAT SPORTS DUDE, JORGE.

CLICK
HE **VOLUNTEERED** TO BE IN A GROUP WITH ME...

NO ONE DOES THAT!

RRING
ENGLISH
...HE LOOKS LIKE HE COULD STOP AN ENTIRE ZOMBIE APOCALYPSE. BY HIMSELF.
...

THAT WAS THE BELL, JORGE. CAN YOU PUT THAT PHONE AWAY?

YES.
SORRY, MISS LEE.
...!

OKAY, EVERYONE, TODAY IS A WORK PERIOD FOR YOUR PRESENTATIONS!
OH NO!!
...THE BASEBALL BOOK!
I COMPLETELY FORGOT TO EVEN FLIP THROUGH IT!

I WANT YOU TO START HAMMERING OUT YOUR SUBTOPICS AND OUTLINE.
I'LL BE WALKING AROUND AND ANSWERING ANY QUESTIONS.

YAMMER CHATTE
HA HA
...
...WHY DIDN'T I EVEN BRING THE BOOK?!

ANY IDEAS FOR A SUBTOPIC?
...!

U-UH.
NOTHING. I GOT NOTHING!

...
UH...
I-I...
...
...ACTUALLY...
...DON'T KNOW MUCH...ABOUT BASEBALL?

...
OH.

OKAY.
WELL...
...BASEBALL'S PRETTY COOL.

RRRIIING

ART CLUB.

...

HA-HA, SINCE WHEN ARE YOU INTO BASEBALL, JENSEN?

BASEBALL for IDIOTS

HELP.
I THOUGHT THEY JUST HIT A BALL WITH A STICK!
BUT THERE ARE ALL THESE RULES!

WELL, ALL YOU REALLY NEED TO KNOW IS THAT GIANTS ARE THE BEST.
UH, NO. DODGERS ARE.

EXCUSE ME?? WHO'S GOT MORE WORLD SERIES TITLES?
TITLE, SHMITLE.
...
...ARGH, I DON'T UNDERSTAND ANY OF THIS.

FIFTEEN MINUTES LATER.
GUH
...STILL...CAN'T...
...UGH.

...I SHOULD DRAW!
IT'S ART CLUB, AFTER ALL.

WHAT IF WE USED THIS FONT?
IS THIS THE LOGO?
...
...OH YEAH, EVERYONE'S WORKING ON THE ARTS FESTIVAL STUFF.

WELL, I'M GOING TO WORK ON...
...
SAVING THE WORLD
(A.K.A. MY SUNSPOTS ARTICLE.)

FIFTEEN MINUTES LATER.
WRITING ARTICLES IS HAAAAARD...
I WISH I COULD JUST MAKE IT INTO A COMIC...

HEY, ARTCLUB
...!

HUFF HUFF
...
UUH.
HI, JENNY.
WHAT'S UP?

...I THOUGHT YOU HATED US NOW?
ugh.
I DO.
traitors.
YOU RUINED OUR LIVES FOR A WEEK.

BUT, UGH, WE HAVE AN EDITING EMERGENCY!!

S-SO I'M HERE, BEING NICE, TO SEE IF ONE OF YOU...
cough deadline-missing jerkfaces *cough*
...CAN HELP US OUT?
...
...

riiiiight...

WELL, WE'RE ALL DOING STUFF FOR THE ARTS FESTIVAL...
...EXCEPT FOR JENSEN.

...JENSEN!
PERFECT.
WE NEED YOU ANYWAY!

O-OKAY!

THERE IS SOMETHING I SHOULD PROBABLY EXPLAIN ABOUT JENNY...

CHAPTER 3

...JENNY BASICALLY HAS THREE SETTINGS.
DASH DASH DAS
COOL AND PROFESSIONAL JENNY...
it just makes sense!
...FREAKING-OUT, FRANTIC JENNY...
FIX IT!
FIX IT!
NO, NO, NO!
...AND THE CURRENT MODE, KNOWN AS...
"DON'T MESS WITH ME FOR I AM THE WRATH OF ANGELS"
APOCALYPSE JENNY!

I WAS REALLY CONFUSED AT FIRST, BECAUSE SHE SWITCHED BETWEEN THEM WITH NO WARNING.
GOT ONE!
HEEEY, SPACEMAN!
OH, JENSEN, YAY!

AKILAH, TELL HIM WHAT TO DO!!
I'M GONNA GET MIC'D UP.
AYE-AYE, CAPTAIN!

THANKS SO MUCH FOR HELPING US, JENSEN.
HOW'S TODAY BEEN FOR YOU?

....!
O-OH!
UH. GOOD! TODAY, I...
NO TIME FOR CHITCHAT, AKILAH!!
UGH, OKAY, OKAY!
COOL YOUR BOSSY PANTS.

...OKAY, BASICALLY, WE NEED AAALL OF THESE PHOTOS FORMATTED.
THERE'S THE FOLDER.

...AND I WROTE YOU THIS STEP-BY-STEP.
AKILAH, WE GOTTA DO THIS—ARE YOU READY?!
I'LL BE RIGHT THERE!

...?
I HOPE THAT HELPS. THANKS AGAIN!!!

C'MON, DUDE, GET YOUR MIC ON!
DON'T "DUDE" ME!
...?

...WAIT.
ARE THEY...?

FELIPE, IS THE PROMPTER READY?
...!
ALMOST!
...THEY ARE!

JENSEN, DON'T GET DISTRACTED. WE NEED THOSE PHOTOS!!!
Y-YES!
...THEY'RE FILMING AN EPISODE OF THEIR SHOW?? I DIDN'T KNOW THEY DID IT HERE!!

READY TO ROLL, FEARLESS LEADER! JUST SAY WHEN!
ARGH, WE'RE LOSING TIME! JUST GO, GO!
•REC
OKAY, ROLLING ON ONE...TWO...
THREE...
...GO.

WELCOME!!
TO THIS WEEK'S EPISODE OF...
BERRY SCOOP!
YOUR LATEST SCOOP ON ALL THINGS BERRYBROOK MIDDLE SCHOOL!
I'M JENNY YAO...
AND I'M AKILAH SALIB!

WITH OUR CAMERA WIZARD, FELIPE...
'SUP.
NEWS ITEM 1!
...AND, BOY, DO WE HAVE BIG NEWS FOR YOU THIS WEEK!

J.Y. SMITH!! J.Y. SMITH!
EEEEEE
AT OUR SCHOOL!!! I AM SO EXCITED! I READ ALL HIS BOOKSSS.

my badly drawn life by J.Y. Smith
VOLUME 5
my badly drawn life THE MOVIE
YES! THIS WORLD-FAMOUS AUTHOR WILL BE A SKYPE GUEST AT OUR SCHOOL'S SPRING ARTS FESTIVAL!
HE WILL BE DOING A READING, A WORKSHOP, AND A Q&A!

NEWS ITEM 2
FACULTY NEWS!!

(x+27)x4 / x+57 = 2
MR. KRISTOFFER BRINGS FORTH THE MATHPOCALYPSE!
WE HAVE REPORTS OF EXTRA HOMEWORK AND TESTS ACROSS ALL GRADES! WATCH OUT!

AND IN LESS DIRE NEWS—
HA HA
78, 79, 80...
WE HAVE SNAGGED EXCLUSIVE FOOTAGE OF MRS. RASHAD CRUSHING MR. AARANSON IN A PUSH-UP COMPETITION!
i give up...
IT WAS THE STUFF OF LEGENDS.

ANY COMMENT FOR BERRY SCOOP, GUYS?
DO IT AGAIN!
DO IT AGAIN!
I WOULD LIKE TO THANK MY FAMILY AND MY AWESOME ARMS.
I'M GOING TO GO AWAY TO TRAIN IN THE MOUNTAINS AND COME BACK FOR A REMATCH.

...DO YOU THINK HE'LL REEEALLY GO AWAY TO TRAIN IN THE MOUNTAINS?
I HOPE SO! THAT WOULD MEAN NO GEOGRAPHY UNTIL HE COMES BACK!

...AND NOW, IT'S TIME TO ANSWER SOME E-MAILS FROM OUR VIEWERS!

AMIRA WRITES, "DEAR BERRY SCOOP—"
...
...
...
...THIS IS SO AWESOME.

I WONDER...
CAN I GET ON THE SHOW?

COMING AT YOU LIVE WITH THE LATEST COVERAGE ON THE DANGER OF SUNSPOTS...
...IT'S JENSEN GRAHAM!
THANK YOU, JENNY. I'M UP HERE IN ZERO-GRAV, MONITORI
CUT!

JENSEN, ARE YOU CROPPING THOSE PHOTOS?
HEY, WANT ME TO DO THAT LAST BIT?
.....!!
Y-YES! YES, I AM!

...OKAY, LET'S TRY THE E-MAILS AGAIN—ONE, TWO...
CLICK
CLICK
CLICK

TIC TOC
TIC
TOC

I NEED SOMEONE TO PROOFREAD THIS!
OK.
JENNY, DO YOU WANT TO CUT THIS BIT?
UH.
JENNY, I THINK I JUST DELETED THE WHOLE FOLDER...?
WHAT?!
...OH, WAIT. NO, HERE IT IS.

TIC TOC TIC TOC

...UPLOADING...
...UPLOADING...
AND...
DONE!!
WITH TWO MINUTES TO SPARE, YOU GUYS!
YESSS! ANOTHER EPISODE OUT ON TIME!
YAAAAAY

...OOF.
...HMM, I GUESS THERE'S NO TIME TO DO JENSEN'S INTERVIEW TODAY...
JUST GIVE HIM THE HANDOUT. HE SHOULD READ THAT FIRST ANYWAY.

OH YEAH, GOOD IDEA!
...?
...INTERVIEW? HANDOUT...?

...WH-WHAT INTERVIEW?
FOR OUR PROJECT. YOU AGREED TO HELP YESTERDAY?
HERE'S SOME INFO ABOUT IT.

READ THIS AND COME BACK NEXT WEEK, 'KAY?

SOCIAL STUDIES PROJECT
THE LIZARD BRAIN CULTURE
in middle school
by
Jenny Yao and Akilah Salib

...LIZARD BRAIN...? WHAAA...

C'MON, GUYS, WE HAVE TO CLEAR OUT!
O-OKAY!

PHEW, WHAT A RACE TODAY...
THANKS FOR HELPING US AGAIN, JENSEN.
...O-OH, ANYTIME!

...ANYTIME?
REEEALLY?
CAREFUL, MAN, SHE'LL GIVE YOU A JOB, HA-HA!
THAT'S HOW SHE GOT ME.

I-I'D BE OKAY WITH THAT!
I LIKE TO HELP.

I WAS HELPING MY MOM WITH A FUND-RAISER, AND THEY SAID I—
SHH, YOU HAD ME AT "I LIKE TO HELP."
GIVE ME YOUR CELL NUMBER. I'LL TEXT YOU IF WE NEED HELP AGAIN.

....!

THE NEXT DAY.
RRING
BERRYBROOK MIDDLE SCHOOL
GLEEEEE!
...I'M PART OF THE NEWSPAPER CREW!!

...WELL, NOT EXACTLY PART OF IT, BUT...
...THEY WANT MY HELP!
JENNY EVEN TOOK MY NUMBER!
BEAM
BEAM

...
...NO TEXT YET.

...
I FEEL LIKE BATMAN, WAITING FOR THE BAT-SIGNAL.

TODAY'S LEVEL—
START!!

MATH.
JENSEN, YOU WILL LEARN MATH IF IT'S THE LAST THING I DO!!
UGHH... nasa... astronaut...

COMPUTERS.
FIELD TRIP SLIPS! DON'T FORGET!
OH, YEAH!

GEOGRAPHY.
...NO, I AM NOT LEAVING TO TRAIN IN THE MOUNTAINS.
SO, YES, YOU DO HAVE TO DO YOUR HOMEWORK!

LUNCH!!

I USED TO HAAATE LUNCH, BECAUSE I'D ALWAYS END UP SITTING ALONE...
IT'S SO DIFFERENT NOW THAT I HAVE ART FRIENDS! WONDER WHAT EVERYONE'S DRAWING TODAY!

HEY, GU...

....!
...HUH?

THAT'S... OUR USUAL TABLE...
...BUT... THOSE'RE NOT MY FRIENDS.

DID THEY...
...SIT SOMEWHERE ELSE?

I DON'T...
SEARCH
SEARCH
...SEE THEM...
...ANYWHERE.

...

. . .
...WHERE'D DID THEY GO?
DID I MISS SOMETHING...?

. . .

FEELS SO WEIRD TO
JUST SIT BY MYSELF.
RRSTLE
...I'M GONNA READ
THAT HANDOUT FROM
JENNY AND AKILAH...

FLIP
FLIP
...WHAT IS THIS LIZARD
BRAIN STUFF?
...THERE'RE SO
MANY PAGES...

. . .
I'LL, UH...
I'LL READ THIS
LATER.

...INSTEAD!! I'LL WORK ON
MY SUNSPOTS ARTICLE!
DIG
DIG
I NEED TO FINISH THAT,
SO I CAN...

...SUBMIT—
HEEY, IS THAT JENSEN?

IT IIIS!
...!
WHERE'RE YOUR NERD FRIENDS? THEY LEFT YOU ALL ALONE?

U-UH...
OF COURSE HE DOES!
WANT *US* TO KEEP YOU COMPANY?
UM.
OOOH, IS THAT YOUR SKETCHBOOK, JENSEN?

HA HA!
YOINK
WHOA!
THAT'S THE WORST-DRAWN *STAR TREK* FANART I'VE EVER SEEN!

...TH-THAT'S NOT... IT'S NOT *STAR TREK*!
IT'S FOR MY SUNSPOTS ARTICLE!
SUNSPOTS?
WHAT'S THAT SUPPOSED—

—TO...
...BE—

CRAP, IT'S JORGE!

IT'S THE FOURTH TIME TODAY!! IS HE FOLLOWING US?
SHF
AGAIN?!

LET'S SIT OVER THERE.
CRAP, NOW THEY'RE ALL COMING OVER?!

WHAT IS THIS, NEIGHBORHOOD WATCH?!! WHAT SHOULD WE DOOOO?
JUST PLAY IT COOL, PLAY IT COOL...

WELL, WELL, WELL...
HEH
IF IT ISN'T THE INCREDIBLE WEASEL DUO!
S-SEAN!
WE WERE JUST LEAVING. DO YOU WANT THIS SEA—?
H-HEY, JORGE! SAVED YOU A SEAT!

PUSH
NAW, SIT.
STAY AWHILE.
HEH HEH
...
...
YO, SEAN. EASY. DIAL IT BACK TO CIVIL.

SIT
CHATTER
OOOH, YOU GUYS GOT PIZZA?
HAHA
CHATTER
SEAN, BACON IS NOT A VEGETABLE.
SAYS WHO?
. . .

HI THERE, NEW GUY!
I'M OLIVIA!
WHAT'S YOUR NAME?

...
U-UH.
JENSEN.
NICE TO MEET YOU, UH JENSEN!
HA HA

S-SO, UH...
...E-EVERYONE SAW THE GAME LAST NIGHT, RIGHT?
HAH! IF YOU CAN CALL THAT A GAME.
...
WHAT IS EVEN HAPPENING RIGHT NOW??

I'M EATING LUNCH WITH THE GAME MONSTERS?!

...
...
WHAT KIND OF BIZARRO ALTERNATE UNIVERSE LEVEL IS THIS?

RRING
CAFETERI

DAZE
WAAA...
...I JUST HEARD MORE ABOUT SPORTS IN ONE HOUR THAN I HAVE IN MY LIFE.

...OLIVIA SAID THEY WERE ALL FROM THE ATHLETICS CLUB.

...I GUESS SPORTS ARE...
...KINDA LIKE THEIR STAR TREK?
HUH.

RRRNG

ART CLUB.
....!
...THERE YOU GUYS ARE!

WHERE'D YOU GO AT LUNCH?
I WAS LOOKING FOR YOU ALL!

OH, THE WEATHER WAS SO NICE, WE WENT AND HAD A PICNIC OUTSIDE.

...A PICNIC!
...I LOVE PICNICS...
DON'T FEEL BAD, JENSEN. THEY DITCHED ME TOO.
WE DITCHED YOU?
YOU'RE THE ONE WHO DITCHED US TO BE WITH YOUR SCIENCE BOYFRIEND!

WH-WHA...?
W-WE'RE JUST WORKING ON A PROJECT TOGETHER!

SURE.
A PROJECT OF... LOOOOVE!
ARGH! NO!
CAN WE FOCUS ON OUR STUFF FOR THE ARTS FESTIVAL, PLEASE?

WE CANNOT SCREW IT UP LIKE WE DID THE COMICS NEWSLETTER, OKAY?
....?
BZZ

....!
...A TEXT FROM JENNY!
SO, JENSEN...
...I KNOW HOW BUMMED YOU WERE ABOUT GETTING LEFT OUT OF THE FESTIVAL PREP...

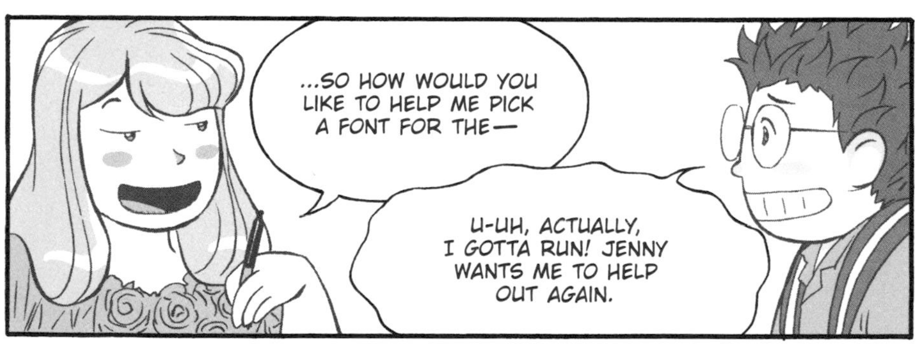
...SO HOW WOULD YOU LIKE TO HELP ME PICK A FONT FOR THE—
U-UH, ACTUALLY, I GOTTA RUN! JENNY WANTS ME TO HELP OUT AGAIN.

BYE!!
....!

...WELL.
ISN'T JENSEN SUDDENLY SPECIAL.

CHAPTER 4

TAPA TAPA TAPA TAP
I AM THE NIGHT.
LIKE A SWIFT SHADOW...

...I COME TO THE RESCUE OF THOSE IN NEED!
JENSEN!!
HUFF HUFF
...HEY, GUYS! YOU CALLED?
♪
PERFECT, COME OVER HERE.

SEE THOSE STACKS? THEY NEED TO BE SORTED TOGETHER AND STAPLED IN THREES, OKAY?
LET ME KNOW IF YOU HAVE QUESTIONS!

...OH.
...
OKAY.

...THIS IS NOT A VERY EXCITING RESCUE.
STAPLE

RUSTLE
H-HEY, WAIT.

THESE PAGES ARE MORE OF THAT LIZARD BRAIN STUFF!

W-WAS I SUPPOSED TO READ THAT FOR TODAY...??
B-BECAUSE I HAVEN'T...

...OKAY, THAT'S DONE! WHAT'S NEXT ON THE TO-DO LIST?
...JENSEN'S HERE—WANNA DO HIS INTERVIEW?
...!
NO! NO, NO...

HMM... NO.
PHEW.
WE STILL HAVE TO FINALIZE THE ARTICLE TOPICS FOR THIS ISSUE.
UGH, I HATE THIS PART.

ARE YOU GOING TO BE DIFFICULT AGAIN?
ONLY IF YOU ARE.

C'MON, JUST ADMIT ALL MY CHOICES ARE **RIGHT**!
MAKE ME.
RUSTLE
STAPLE

ALL YOUR CHOICES ARE TOO **SAFE**!
YOU TOTALLY CUT ALL THE **IMPORTANT** STUFF!
PFFFT, I DO NOT.
...LIKE WHAT?

LIKE MY DRAMA CLUB STORY IDEA!
WE NEED TO PRINT SOMETHING ABOUT THAT!

...DRAMA IN A MIDDLE SCHOOL DRAMA CLUB— ARE YOU SERIOUS?
THAT'S JUST GOSSIP. IT'S NOT—
STAPLE
RUSTLE
NO, NO, NO!
TEACHER FAVORITISM IN A MIDDLE SCHOOL DRAMA CLUB! **NEPOTISM**, JENNY!

STAPLE
RUSTLE
...
...
...WH-WHAT'S "NEPOTISM"?

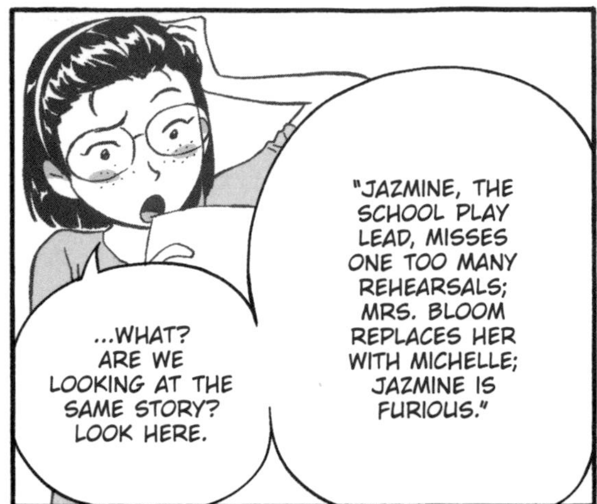
"JAZMINE, THE SCHOOL PLAY LEAD, MISSES ONE TOO MANY REHEARSALS; MRS. BLOOM REPLACES HER WITH MICHELLE; JAZMINE IS FURIOUS."
...WHAT? ARE WE LOOKING AT THE SAME STORY? LOOK HERE.

STUPID BUT FAIR. WHERE DO YOU SEE NEPOTISM?
OKAY, FIRST?
JAZMINE ONLY MISSED ONE REHEARSAL...
...BECAUSE HER MOM WAS IN THE HOSPITAL.

AND SECOND?
MICHELLE? SHE'S MRS. BLOOM'S RICH COUSIN'S NIECE.

THEY'RE... FAMILY?
YES!
AND MRS. BLOOM HAS A HISTORY OF GIVING RICH KIDS BETTER ROLES SO THAT THEIR PARENTS GIVE MONEY TO THE PRODUCTION!

HOW IS THAT FAIR?
JAZMINE WORKED HER HEART OUT FOR THAT ROLE!
AND SHE DOESN'T GET TO PLAY IT BECAUSE HER FAMILY'S NOT RICH!

WE HAVE TO RUN SOMETHING ABOUT THIS!
HMM...
THAT'D BE QUITE AN ACCUSATION.

WE HAVE TO...
...CONSULT THE ORACLE.

WAIT, WHAT? WAIT, WAAAIT, NO...
DO WE HAVE TO?
YES.
THIS IS BIG.

Z Z Z
. . .
ORACLE.
...SHE'S SLEEPING AGAIN.

....!
SHAKE
SHAKE
C'MON, MRS. CRABBLER, WAKE UP!! WE HAVE A QUESTION!
...*snork* retirement?...

NO, YOU'RE NOT RETIRED YET! PLEASE WAKE UP!
wha...
HMPF
so noisy...

...WHAT?
WHAT IS THIS MESS?
...HUH?
THAT'S JUST OUR RESEARCH. IT'S NOT—

YOU HAVE TO ALWAYS ORGANIZE YOUR RESEARCH, LADIES!

LET ME SHOW YOU HOW BEST TO.
NO! NONONO WE JUST HAVE ONE QUESTION

...AN ORGANIZED DESK MAKES FOR AN ORGANIZED MIND!
NOOOOOOOOOOoo
JUST ONE QUESTION
STOP!! ARGH

TWO HOURS LATER.
THERE.
SPARKLE SPARKLE
NOW THEN, WHAT WAS YOUR QUESTION?

...
IT'S LATE, AND WE HAVE TO GO HOME NOW.

...WHY DO YOU CALL HER "THE ORACLE"?
BECAUSE SHE TELLS US WHAT WE CAN AND CAN'T PUBLISH...
UGH, WE JUST LOST AN ENTIRE AFTERNOON!
JENSEN, DID YOU AT LEAST FINISH STAPLING THE SURVEYS?

YES, I DID!!
OH, GOOD.
AND I FINISHED THE ROUGH CUT OF THE OUTTAKES!
YOU DID?!

THANKS, YOU GUYS! YOU'RE LIFESAVERS!
TOMORROW, WE TRY, TRY AGAIN!

..."WE"?
DOES...DOES THAT MEAN ME TOO...?
MAYBE...?

RRRING

...IT DID.
IT DID MEAN ME!
BERRYBROOK MID
IT'S BEEN A COUPLE OF WEEKS NOW...

PING!
...BUT I STILL GET TEXTS FROM JENNY TO COME HELP.

IT'S MOSTLY SMALL STUFF...
YOU GUYS CALLED?
JENSEN! YEAH! THESE NEED FOLDING.
...BUT I DON'T CARE...

♪
FOLD FOLD
...BECAUSE THEN I'M PART OF THE CREW!
(KINDA, SORTA...)

...IT'S NICE I CAN GO THERE...
...BECAUSE ART CLUB IS NOT AS FUN AS IT USED TO BE...
bicker bicker
HI, GU—
ugh!
WHY IS THE DATE WRONG?! YOU WERE SUPPOSED TO CHECK IT!
NO, YOU WERE!

JENSEN, YOU'RE IN THE WAY!
MOVE MOVE
sorry, sorry!!

...I TRY NOT TO BUG THEM TOO MUCH.
O-OKAY, I'LL JUST BE IN THE BACK.

...MATH IS STILL EVIL, UGH...
...EVERYONE, HAND IN YOUR PRACTICE TESTS NOW!
THAT MEANS YOU TOO, JENSEN!
ALMOST... DONE...
LAST... QUESTION...

...AND THERE IS STILL THE USUAL DAILY GAUNTLET.
HEY JENSEEEN!
....!
NO NO NO

BUT NOW, THE PRIZE AT THE END IS...
PING!
...THE NEWSPAPER!

THEY ARE SO BUSY, I THINK THEY FORGOT ABOUT THAT LIZARD BRAIN INTERVIEW...
COME ON, COME ON, CLOCK'S TICKING!

...WHICH IS GOOD, BECAUSE I STILL HAVEN'T READ THAT HANDOUT.

...WE'RE GOING TO BARRICADE OURSELVES IN HERE.

GROWL
BANG
SNARL

WE HAVE TO RATION THESE SNACKS, YOU GUYS.

SPLIT THEM FOUR WAYS.

THREE. I DON'T NEED ANY.

BUT, JENSEN, YOU'LL STARVE!

NOPE. I'VE GOT A PROTEIN BAR AND THIS!

PROTEIN

ZOMBIE SURVIVAL GUIDE

WE'RE GONNA BE OKAY.

JENSEN! NO DAYDREAMING!
TICK-TOCK!

I'M ALSO GETTING TO KNOW THE NEWSPAPER CREW BETTER.

AKILAH LOOOOVES JOURNALISM. SHE'S CONSTANTLY REPORTING SOMETHING.
RRING RRING
HELLO, BERRYBROOK PD? I'M FROM A LOCAL PAPER CALLING FOR COMMENT ABOUT THE VANDAL CASE.
HER DREAM IS TO WORK FOR THE NEW YORK TIMES.

JENNY'S ~~DREAM~~ LIFE GOAL IS TO **RUN** IT.
SHRUG
...OR START MY OWN MEDIA EMPIRE. WE'LL SEE.

FELIPE'S CURRENT GOAL IS TO SEE HOW MANY STAIRS HE CAN JUMP AT ONCE ON HIS SKATEBOARD.
GONNA FLY LIKE AN EAGLE, YO.

...THOUGH, SOMETIMES, GETTING TO KNOW THEM GETS, UH...AWKWARD...
...HEY, DON'T HATE ME JUST BECAUSE I'M RIGHT!
...
...BECAUSE JENNY AND AKILAH FIGHT.
LIKE, A LOT.
UGH, YOU'RE SO BOSSY!

...
IF BY "BOSSY" YOU MEAN "AWESOME."
BY "BOSSY" I MEAN "WE'RE NO LONGER FRIENDS"!

LATER.
HA HA HA
THEY'RE TOTALLY STILL FRIENDS.
THOSE TWO? OH, YEAH, HA-HA! THEY'RE, LIKE, SUPERGLUED TOGETHER.
THEY JUST FRIEND-FIGHT LIKE IT'S A SPORT.

UGH, STOP BEING STUPID, JENSEN.
...FRIEND-FIGHT!
IS THAT WHAT TESSA AND I DO?

RRRING
BERRYBROOK M
ANOTHER SCHOOL DAY...
START

JENSEN, STOP DRAWING SPACESHIPS AND PAY ATTENTION!
H-HOW DOES HE KNOW?!

I WILL NOW RETURN YOUR PRACTICE TESTS FROM YESTERDAY!

LETICIA, GOOD JOB.
JANE, YOU CAN DO BETTER.
NATHANIEL, SOLID EFFORT.
JENSEN.
...
...?

F
STAY TO SEE ME AFTER CLASS.

!?
I *FAILED*?! BUT I USUALLY AT LEAST SCRAPE BY...

RRING
YAMMER
CHATTER
Y-YOU...
...WANTED TO SEE ME?

JENSEN, IS EVERYTHING OKAY AT HOME?

...HUH?
IS YOUR MOM STILL ABLE TO HELP YOU WITH HOMEWORK?

...OH.
UM. NO...
SH-SHE GOT MOVED TO A LATER SHIFT... AND OVERTIME... S-SO...

I SEE.
...

TAKKA TAK
ALL RIGHT, THEN I'M SIGNING YOU UP FOR MY TUTORING GROUP.
TAKKA
...!
WE MEET EVERY DAY AFTER SCHOOL IN THIS ROOM.
YOU'LL START TODAY.

T-TODAY?!
BUT I HAVE ART CLUB! A-AND NEWSPAPER!

JENSEN, YOU'RE IN DANGER OF FAILING THIS CLASS.

THEY'LL HAVE TO SPARE YOU FOR A WHILE.

ENGLISH CLASS
(WORK PERIOD AT THE LIBRARY.)
GLOOM
...
...

...
DUDE, DID YOUR DOG DIE OR SOMETHING?

...
I-I...
I'm failing math...
...and...I have to...
...go to a... ...a tutoring group...
...instead of art club...
AH.
...
BUMMER.

...TUTORING'S GOOD THOUGH.
I GOT SOME FOR SCIENCE. REALLY SAVED MY BUTT.

R-REALLY?
YEAH. THAT STUFF, LIKE, MAKES SENSE NOW.

HUH! MAYBE IT WON'T BE SO BAD.
...
THOUGH, I'LL STILL BE MISSING ART CLUB...
I'M WORRIED MY ART FRIENDS MIGHT FORGET ABOUT ME...AGAIN...

. . .
...THEY **FORGET** ABOUT YOU?
...THOSE DON'T SOUND LIKE FRIENDS.

NO, NO, IT'S NOT LIKE THAT! THEY'RE JUST... BUSY. LOTS TO DO...

. . .

...IF THEY'RE FRIENDS, THEN THEY'VE GOT YOUR BACK...
...WHETHER YOU'RE THERE OR NOT.
. . .
FRIENDS WON'T "FORGET" ABOUT YOU.

...OH.

RRING
LIBRARY

*JORGE IS **SO COOL**.*
LATER.
BYE!

HE'S ALWAYS SUPER NICE...
...AND I NOTICED THAT—

...IS THERE A PROBLEM HERE?
—HE'S KINDA LIKE THE SCHOOL SHERIFF.

HIM AND OLIVIA BOTH, ALWAYS LOOKING OUT FOR PEOPLE...
ARE YOU OKAY?
SNFFL
...
KEEP WALKING, BUDDY.
...I WONDER IF THEY'D WANT TO BE ON MY ZOMBIE SURVIVAL TEAM...
RAWR
RAWR
RAWR

. . .
...THE NEWSPAPER CREW! WHO'RE THEY TALKING TO?

...AH!
HEY, JENSEN!

NEED YOU TO COME OVER AGAIN TODAY AFTER SCHOOL.
WE'RE FINALLY DOING YOUR INTERVIEW, SO DON'T BE LATE.

...INTERVIEW?!
. . . !
I STILL HAVEN'T READ THAT HANDOUT!!

U-UH!
A-ACTUALLY...
...I CAN'T!
TODAY...
...I HAVE MATH TUTORING?

OH.
UHHH, OKAY...
HOW ABOUT TOMORROW, DURING LUNCH...?
CAN YOU COME THEN?

YESSS,
I'LL BE
THERE!

...TOMORROW AT LUNCH?
THIS SHOULD TOTALLY GIVE ME
ENOUGH TIME TO READ IT...

RRRRING
...BUT BEFORE TOMORROW...
NEWSPAP
ART CLU
MATH TUTORING
...I STILL HAVE TO MAKE IT THROUGH
TODAY'S SURPRISE BONUS LEVEL.

I SURE HOPE
JORGE'S RIGHT...

...AND THIS WILL
HELP SAVE MY BUTT.
H-HELLO?
AH, JENSEN!
GOOD,
YOU MADE IT.

YOU'RE IN GROUP TWO TODAY, AND YOUR TUTOR IS AARON.
THAT'S ME!
HEY.

WHATEVER QUESTIONS AARON CAN'T ANSWER, YOU CAN ASK ME.
GO AHEAD AND MEET YOUR GROUP.

SO, JENSEN, RIGHT? HAVE YOU EVER BEEN IN A TUTORING GROUP BEFORE?
UH, NO...

WELL, WE DON'T BITE.
...!
WELL, MAYBE YANIC DOES.

BUT HE IS OFF-DUTY AND LEARNING MATH, LIKE EVERYONE ELSE.
....!
JENSEN?!

UH.

CHAPTER 5

RUSTLE RUSTLE
OH, WHOOPS, I FORGOT THE WORK SHEETS.

BE RIGHT BACK!
....!

. . .
THIS IS SO WEIRD.
SHOULD I SAY SOMETHING?

UH...
H-HELLO.
HOW'S IT GOING?
....!

...
FINE.
WHATEVER.
TWRL

TWRL

...HOW ARE YOU DOING THAT?
...WHA—?
OH.
I DUNNO.
IT'S PRETTY EASY.

FLING

. . .
. . .

ALL RIGHT, HERE THEY ARE!
WHO'S READY TO LEARN SOME MATH?

WHY IS YANIC BEING SO WEIRD?
MAYBE THIS TUTORING THING WASN'T SUCH A GOOD IDEA...

...ON THE OTHER HAND, WOW, AARON'S REALLY GOOD AT EXPLAINING.
OHHH.

...EVEN YANIC'S LISTENING.
!

...THOUGH, VICKIE SEEMS REALLY DISTRACTED.
...
TWRL
WHY'S SHE HERE ANYWAY? I THOUGHT SHE HAD GOOD MARKS?

...
...WOW, MY HOMEWORK MAKES SENSE FOR THE FIRST TIME IN MONTHS.

BEAM

BLEAHH

YANIC, JENSEN, THIS IS NOT A TONGUE-MEASURING CONTEST! ROLL THOSE BACK UP!

SEE YOU GUYS
SAME TIME
TOMORROW!
THANKS,
AARON!

...
...

SEE YOU
DON'T
TALK
TO ME.

...
...I WISH THERE WAS
TUTORING FOR MIDDLE SCHOOL
LIFE...BECAUSE THAT STILL
DOESN'T MAKE SENSE.

RRRING
BERRYBROOK MIDD

BLAH
BLAH
BLAH
BLAH
BLAH
3/16 = 0.1875
I'M PRETTY EXCITED
ABOUT TUTORING NOW.

NASA MARS PROGRAM, HERE I COME!!
HMM, STRANDED ON MARS...
IT'S A GOOD THING I KNOW HOW TO GROW POTATOES IN POOP.
THANK YOU, THE MARTIAN.
AND ONCE I'M AT NASA, SAVING THE WORLD FROM SUNSPOTS WILL BE SO—
JENSEN, WILL YOU FOCUS, PLEASE?!
RRING
YAMMER CHATTER
...A TEXT FROM JENNY!
DON'T FORGET!! LUNCH AT NEWSPAPER OFFICE!! INTERVIEW.
...OH YEAH, THAT'S RIGHT!

I GOTTA READ THAT LIZARD BRAIN THING!

....!
HA HA HAHA

...NOOO, I NEED TO GO THAT WAY!
WHY AREN'T THEY GOING TO CLASS?!

I'LL HAVE TO GO AROUND.

HAHAHAHA
....!
...NO!

GAME MONSTERS BOTH WAYS?

UH... UH...
...

...W-WELL, WE'VE BEEN... IN TUTORING GROUP TOGETHER...
...SO MAYBE...
...THIS WAY?

WELL, LOOK WHO IT IS!
DUMBO THE SCIENTIST!

ARGH, WRONG CHOICE!
IS IT TRUE THAT YOU NEED TUTORING?
I THOUGHT YOU NERDS ARE SUPPOSED TO BE SMART!

U-UM.
I HAVE TO GO.
AW, COME ON, STAY AND CHAT!
GRAB

...OH! JORGE! THERE YOU ARE!
TURN

NEW DEFENSE STRATEGY—UNLOCKED!

...OKAY, OKAY. HERE GOES.
"THE HUMAN BRAIN IS A COMPLEX SYSTEM OF CELLS AND NEURAL CONNECTIONS WHICH ARE STILL NOT WELL-UNDERSTOOD.
...
...UH.
RIGHT.

"FOR EXAMPLE, WHILE THE R-COMPLEX IS RESPONSIBLE FOR BASIC SURVAaaaa
I CAN'T. I CAN'T READ THIS IN TEN MINUTES.

FLIP FLIP FLIP
WHY ARE THERE SO MANY PAGES...?

ZARD BRAIN INSTIN
• TERRITORIALITY, HOARDING OF RESOURCES
RRR! MINE! NO TOUCHIE!
• AGGRESSION, DOMINANCE
I AM BE ST!! BOW TO ME!!
• FEAR/SELF-DEF
OH HEY, WHAT'S THIS?

NSTINCTS
• AGGRESSION, DOMINANCE
I AM BE ST!! BOW TO ME!!
HA-HA, THIS ANGRY ONE LOOKS LIKE YANIC!

....!
DING
BZZ
JENSEN, WHERE ARE YOU?!

DASH!

JENSEN!!
FINALLY!!
S-SORRY!

GET OVER THERE!
FELIPE, MIC HIM UP!
AKILAH, DO YOU HAVE THE QUESTIONS?

YES, YES, CAPTAIN McBOSSY.
WE ONLY HAVE TWENTY MINUTES LEFT!!
HOLD STILL.
SH-SHOULD I TELL THEM THAT I DIDN'T READ THE—

...TOO LATE.
REC
ROLL IT!
12
THIS IS CASE STUDY NUMBER TWELVE...
...FOR "BULLYING CULTURE: THE LIZARD BRAIN SABOTAGE OF CIVILIZED SOCIETY."

"LIZARD BRAIN SABOTAGE"?
...
STUDY PARTICIPANT IS TWELVE-YEAR-OLD JENSEN GRAHAM, VICTIM OF BULLYING.

HUH?
DOES SHE MEAN ME?
JENSEN, CAN YOU SHARE SOME EXAMPLES HOW LIZARD BRAIN BEHAVIORS AFFECT YOUR DAILY LIFE?

...
U-UH.

...I CAN'T. I HAVE TO CONFESS.
U-UM.
WH-WHAT'S LIZARD BRAIN?
I, UH, I DIDN'T ACTUALLY READ THE... THE THING?

...
YOU...
YOU...DIDN'T?
YOU DIDN'T READ...

YOU DIDN'T READ IT?!!
...!!
YOU HAD WEEKS, JENSEN!!! WE SET EVERYTHING UP FOR—

—THIS INTERVIEW AND YOU—
SIGH...
BETTER STOP THE RECORDING, FELIPE.
...SO, JENSEN, WHAT JENNY IS CURRENTLY EXHIBITING IS A LIZARD BRAIN REACTION.
ALSO SOME SPECIAL EFFECTS.

INSTEAD OF RATIONAL PROBLEM-SOLVING, JENNY HAS REACTED WITH RAGE...
GLARE
...A PRIMAL DEFENSE MECHANISM AGAINST DISTURBANCE OF CONTROL OF ONE'S ENVIRONMENT.
STOPPIT, JENNY, 'KAY?
WHAT

THIS IS NOT RAGE THIS IS RIGHTEOUS INDIGNAT
J-JENNY HAS A LIZARD BRAIN??!
NO! UH...
WELL, UM...
OH BOY...

UM, OKAY, SO...UH...
THE THEORY WE ARE EXPLORING HERE IS THAT EVERY HUMAN IS BORN WITH, LIKE, A PRERECORDED SET OF SURVIVAL INSTINCTS, RIGHT?
REALLY BASIC STUFF LIKE—
"HUNGRY! FIND FOOD!" OR "DANGER! ACTIVATE DEFENSE MODE. UGH!"

grumble
GLARE
...LIKE YOU'RE DOING RIGHT NOW. "DANGER! ANGRY JENNY! STAY AWAY!"
ACCORDING TO OUR RESEARCH, EVERYONE HAS THESE BASIC SURVIVAL REACTIONS SINCE FOREVER.
WE'RE CALLING THAT THE "LIZARD" OR "TROGLODYTIC" BRAIN.
RAWR

AND EVEN THOUGH HUMANS ALSO HAVE *HIGHER* BRAIN FUNCTIONS—
—STUFF THAT LETS US CREATE ART, BUILD AMAZING THINGS, FLY SPACESHIPS—

—THE TROGLODYTIC BRAIN IS STILL THERE TOO!!! SENDING ALL SORTS OF "HEY! DO THIS TO SURVIVE!" SIGNALS.

BULLYING IS A TROGLODYTIC TACTIC! TRYING TO GET POWER BY PUSHING EVERYONE DOWN, TO SHOW HOW "TOP DOG" YOU ARE.
...THAT'S WHAT JENNY WAS BASICALLY ASKING YOU. "HOW DOES BEING BULLIED AFFECT YOUR LIFE?"

...!
OHHHH!

S-SO...
...LET'S TRY THIS AGAIN.
HOW DOES BEING BULLIED AFFECT YOUR LIFE, JENSEN?
O-OH, ACTUALLY, I'M NOT?
BEING BULLIED?

WHAT?
YES. YES, YOU ARE.
THEY'RE CONSTANTLY HARASSING YOU.
TWITCH
OH, NO, NO!
THEY'VE NEVER CAUGHT ME! I'M TOO FAST!

...DUDE, THEY CALL YOU **NAMES**. THAT'S VERBAL BULLYING.
...!

UH...
WELL...

"STICKS AND STONES CAN BREAK MY BONES, BUT WORDS WILL NEVER HURT ME!"
AAAAAA
...!

...JENSEN, WORDS CAN ***TOTALLY*** HURT YOU.
WORDS
SAVE YOUR BREATH, LADY.
I'M GONNA GIVE HIM THE BULLYING CULTURE SURVEY.

JENSEN, IT HAS AN INFO SHEET TOO, ON THE THREE TYPES OF BULLYING.
I'M NOT...
THEY'RE ***WRONG****.*

READ IT, PLEASE.
THEN FILL OUT THE SURVEY AND COME BACK MONDAY, OKAY?
O-OKAY...
RRRING

...THAT WAS SO WEIRD. LIZARD BRAIN? TROGOL...
...TROGLODYTIC.

...OH, IT HAS THOSE CARTOONS AGAIN!

LIZARD BRAIN
• TERRITORIALITY, HOARDING OF RESOURCES
RRR! MINE!
• AGGRESSION, DOMINANCE
I AM BEST!! BOW TO ME!!
EAR/SELF-DEFENSE
HA-HA, IT STILL LOOKS LIKE YANIC!

...OH.
HERE'S THE SURVEY.

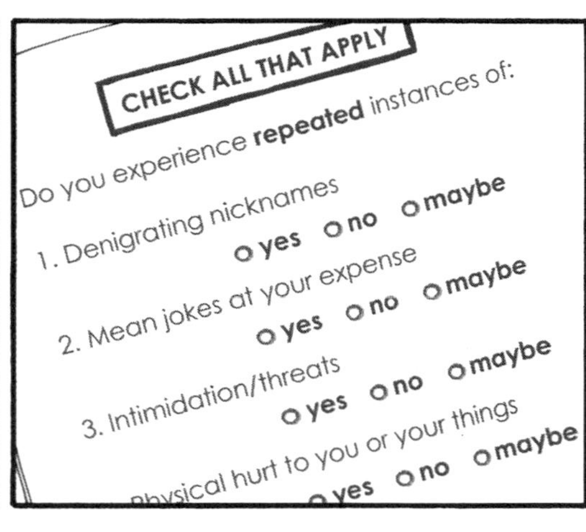
CHECK ALL THAT APPLY
Do you experience **repeated** instances of:
1. Denigrating nicknames
yes no maybe
2. Mean jokes at your expense
yes no maybe
3. Intimidation/threats
yes no maybe
Physical hurt to you or your things
yes no maybe

TH-THESE DON'T APPLY TO ME...

HA HA CHATTER HE
...
...DO THEY?

COMPUTER CLASS.
TAKA TAKA TAK
...

BAND CLASS.

AFTER SCHOOL, HALLWAY.
HAHA
edge edge

...I WAS RIGHT!
AS LONG AS I'M CAREFUL, EVERYTHING'S FINE!

PEOPLE JUST **IGNORE** ME, SO THAT'S A "NO" FOR ALL THESE QUES—

OH! THERE'S ONE MORE PAGE.

12. Do you have someone who will save a seat for you? Or do you feel isolated/left out?
o yes o no o maybe

. . .

HA HA HA
. . .
o you have someone who will
ave a seat for you?
Or do you feel isolated/left out
yes no
left out?
maybe

MATH TUTORING GROUP.
Be back in 15 min — Mr. K.
WHAT A WEIRD LEVEL TODAY...
SO TIRED NOW. WANNA GO HOME.

SLAM

HEY, DUMBO.
SIT
FUNNY JOKE ABOUT JORGE TODAY.

DID YOU COME UP WITH THAT YOURSELF, OR DID HE WRITE IT FOR YOU?
...AAAND YANIC IS BACK TO HIS OLD SELF.

HEY.
HEY.
ARE YOU GONNA SAY SOMETHING?
NOPE!

OKAY, LOOKS LIKE VICKIE DIDN'T MAKE IT TODAY...
LET'S GO AHEAD AND START.
HEEEY, IT'S THE AMAZING BIONIC MAN!
HALF MAN, HALF CRUTCH!

...!
HA.
HA.
REAL CLASSY, YANIC.

THESE ARE TODAY'S WORK SHEETS. WE'LL START WITH THESE SAMPLES—
FLIP
FLIP

...YEAH, YEAH, YEAH.
OKAY.
BUT HOW ABOUT...

...WE DO *MY* HOMEWORK FIRST? I GOT A BASEBALL GAME TO GET TO.
....!

...UH, NO.
JENSEN IS MISSING HIS ACTIVITIES TOO. IT WOULDN'T BE FAIR.

NOW, LET'S TURN TO PAGE ONE.
...

Be back in 15 min— Mr. K.
...

LISTEN, NERDS.
SLAM

I GOT PLACES TO BE. SO MY HOMEWORK? MAKE IT HAPPEN.

• AGGRESSION, DOMINANCE
I AM BEST!! BOW TO ME!!
...!
L-LIZARD BRAIN...

...!
...WHAT'D YOU CALL ME?!

U-UH...
NOTHING.
I HEARD YOU! YOU CALLED ME A LIZARD BRAIN, YOU...

...FATSO!
YANIC!! THAT'S QUITE ENOUGH!

....!
HE STARTED IT!! HE CALLED ME A LIZARD BRAIN!
YOU ARE DISRUPTING THE GROUP, YANIC...
... AGAIN.

MOVE YOUR THINGS TO MY DESK.
I WILL BE YOUR GROUP.
....!

THIS...FEELS LIKE IT WON'T END WELL.
. . .
GLARE

CHAPTER 6

RRING
BERRYBROOK MI LE SCHOOL
THE NEXT DAY.

WHY DOES MATH HAVE TO BE SO HARD...
...AND WHY DOES YANIC HAVE TO BE THERE?

...AT LEAST ENGLISH IS GOING WELL.
HI, MISS LEE!
GOOD MORNING, JENSEN.
HI, JORGE!
'SUP.
RRING
OKAY, EVERYONE, TODAY IS ANOTHER WORK PERIOD FOR YOUR GROUP PRESENTATIONS, SO USE IT WELL!

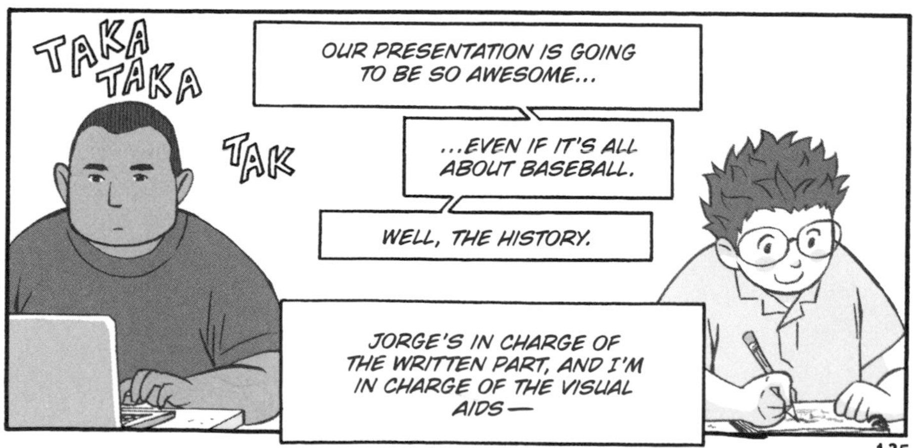
TAKA TAKA
TAK
OUR PRESENTATION IS GOING TO BE SO AWESOME...
...EVEN IF IT'S ALL ABOUT BASEBALL.
WELL, THE HISTORY.
JORGE'S IN CHARGE OF THE WRITTEN PART, AND I'M IN CHARGE OF THE VISUAL AIDS—

DRAWINGS OF SOCIALLY HISTORICAL BASEBALL MOMENTS...

...LIKE THE FIRST AFRICAN-AMERICAN PLAYERS, THE FIRST LADY PLAYERS...

MOSES FLEETWOOD "FLEET" WALKER

BUD FOWLER

ELIZABETH "LIZZIE" MURPHY

TONI STONE

I DIDN'T KNOW PEOPLE WERE SUCH JERKS TO THEM!

I HAVE TO DRAW THOSE PEOPLE TOO, THE ONES WHO WERE EVIL AND HARASSED THE PLAYERS.

I DON'T LIKE THAT PART.

I'M MAKING THEM LOOK EXTRA EVIL SO THAT NO ONE GETS CONFUSED.

RRING
I WONDER IF I CAN BE AN ASTRONAUT…
BEAM BEAM
…AND AN ARTIST?!
…JUST BACK FROM HIS DARING SUNSPOT-FIGHTING MISSION…
…NASA ASTRONAUT JENSEN GRAHAM IS SIGNING COPIES OF HIS NEWEST GRAPHIC NOVEL —
A FIRSTHAND ACCOUNT OF MARTIAN VISTAS, THE STORMS OF JUPITER, AND THE MYSTERIOUS ICE FORMATIONS ON —
MY SPACE ADVENTURES
a captain's logs

YAMM
CHATTE
...HUH? WHY'S THERE A CROWD HERE?

ARTS FESTIVAL
AUTHORS! CONTESTS! PRIZES!
J.Y. SMITH!
SKYPE
INA CRUZ!

...!
J.Y. SMITH?!
AT OUR SCHOOL?!
ME TOO!!
NO WAY!
I READ ALL HIS BOOKS!!!
...OH!! THEY FINISHED THE POSTER!

...THE FESTIVAL IS SO SOON!!
J.Y. SMITH...
INA CRUZ...

I STILL DON'T KNOW WHO ALL THOSE AUTHORS ARE.

LUNCH.
LIBRARY

JENSEN... JENSEN...
TAKA
TAKA
AH! YOU'RE NEXT ON THE WAITING LIST!

COME BACK IN A COUPLE OF DAYS. WE SHOULD HAVE A FEW COPIES RETURNED BY THEN.
...

YUSSSS.

RRRRING
I'M GOING TO READ ALL THOSE BOOKS...
CAFETERI
...AND WHEN PEOPLE AT ART CLUB TALK ABOUT THEM, I'LL BE ABLE TO JOIN IN!

HEY, GUYS, GUESS WHAT!
WHOA, HEY, WHAT ARE YOU DOING?

HUH...?
SITTING... DOWN?
NO!
I'M SAVING THIS SEAT FOR PEPPI!

SHOO, GO FIND ANOTHER SEAT!

...
BUT...

...THERE ISN'T ANOTHER ONE...

PEPPI'S NOT COMING, TESS!
SHE'S WORKING ON THE "PROJECT" WITH HER "NOT-BOYFRIEND."
UGH, WHAT?!
AGAIN?

SO JENSEN CAN SIT THERE, RIGHT?
UGH, I GUESS.

...
ANYWAY, GUYS, WHAT'RE YOU MOST EXCITED FOR AT THE FESTIVAL?!

J.Y. SMITH, DUH.
THE ART CONTEST!
NO, NO, GUYS. THE **COSTUME** CONTEST.

WE CAN DRESS UP AGAIN!! IT'S LIKE A SECOND HALLOWEEN!
I KNOW, RIGHT?! NINA AND I ARE GONNA GO AS...

...DISNEY WARRIOR PRINCESSES!
WE'RE GONNA SLAY SO HARD.

OH, WE'LL SEE ABOUT THAT.
I'M GONNA WEAR MY ***SAILOR SUNBURST*** COSPLAY.
YOUR WHA...?
YEAH, YOU HEARD ME.
THE ONE THAT'S GOT ***RIBBONS*** FOR THE FIRE EFFECTS.
I'M ***SO*** GONNA WIN.

WH-WHO'S SAILOR SU—
OH, ONLY THE BEST ***SAILOR SCOUT*** EVER.
HER SPECIAL ATTACK'S A GIANT FIREBALL.

ARE YOU GONNA DRESS UP, JENSEN?
...OH!
UH, YES! I'M GONNA BE—

WAIT, WAIT!
I'M A PSYCHIC AND WILL READ YOUR MIND...
YOU WILL BE...

...AN ASTRONAUT? WITH A CARDBOARD BOX HELMET.
HA HA

UGH, DON'T BE STUPID, NATHANIEL.

HE'S GONNA GO AS A ***SUNSPOT***, DUH, DRESSED IN, LIKE, A GARBAGE BAG.
...
HA
HA

HA HA HA HA
OMG, YES, JENSEN IS A SUNSPOT!!
HA HA HA HA
Ha...
Ha-ha...
HE'S TOTALLY BIG ENOUGH TO BLOCK OUT THE SUN
...THIS FEELS WEIRD.

GUYS, STOP BEING JERKS.
GEEZ.
HA HA HA HA
BUT IT'S FUNNY!
CHILL OUT, FELICITY.

JENSEN, YOU OKAY?
...
Y-YEAH!
YEAH...THEY'RE JUST JOKING.
WELL, DON'T LET 'EM RIDE YOU.
RRRING
...AT LEAST I THINK THEY ARE JOKING.

BULLYING CULTURE SURVEY

!
...
..."REPEATED CASES OF DISMISSIVE AND MEAN JOKES AT YOUR EXPENSE."

BUT...
...IT'S OKAY IF THEY'RE MY FRIENDS...
...RIGHT?

. . .
. . .

...I WISH THEY WOULDN'T THOUGH.
...MAKE FUN OF ME LIKE THAT.

HEE
HEEHEE

BONK
HA
HA
HA
HA

MONDAY, LUNCH.

UM, I...
I HAVE A QUESTION.
YEAH?
THE, UH... "MEAN AND DISMISSIVE JOKES" PART...

IT DOESN'T COUNT IF IT'S FROM *FRIENDS*, RIGHT?
...WHAT?
ARE YOU SERIOUS...?

IT *TOTALLY* COUNTS. IT COUNTS FOR *MORE*, BECAUSE THEY'RE SUPPOSED TO BE YOUR FRIENDS!
...JENSEN, WHA...?
ARE YOUR *FRIENDS* SAYING MEAN THINGS TO YOU TOO?

u-uh...
well...
N-NO!
THEY'RE... THEY'RE JUST JOKING.

. . .

DUDE, UH...
IF THEY SAY MEAN CRAP ABOUT YOU JUST FOR KICKS AND LAUGHS...

...ARE YOU **SURE** THEY'RE YOUR **FRIENDS**?
. . . !

OKAY, ENOUGH EXPLAINING. WE GOTTA DO THE INTERVIEW— WE'RE SO BEHIND SCHEDULE ALREADY.
. . .
WHY WOULD HE SAY...

AKILAH, DO YOU HAVE THE QUESTIONS?
FELIPE, MIC HIM UP, PLEASE!
OF...OF COURSE THEY'RE MY FRIENDS!

OVER HERE, JENSEN!
...AREN'T THEY?

•REC
12
OKAY, THIS IS TAKE TWO!
INTERVIEW WITH JENSEN GRAHAM, STUDY PARTICIPANT TWELVE!

JENSEN, YOU JUST MENTIONED THAT EVEN YOUR FRIENDS HARASS YOU.
CAN YOU TELL US HOW THAT AFFECTS YOUR LIFE?

U-UH.

...
...

...
Um, is...
Is this going to be on Berry Scoop?
Will the whole school see—
WHAT? NO, NO!

THIS IS JUST FOR OUR PROJECT.
ONLY OUR TEACHER WILL SEE IT.

... A TEACHER?!
UH, YEAH.
...!

UH...
COULD...
...
COULD WE SKIP THAT QUESTION?
I'M NOT...

...JENSEN, ALL THE OTHER QUESTIONS ARE LIKE THIS.
IT'S OUR *TOPIC!*

...O-OH.
...
UH.

...JENSEN, UGH...
I SHOULD'VE ASKED THIS AT THE BEGINNING—
GUH
—ARE YOU OKAY TALKING ABOUT YOUR EXPERIENCES...

...ON **CAMERA**?
•REC

IT'S OKAY TO SAY NO, JENSEN...
U-UH...
...IF YOU'RE NOT OKAY.

...
...
I...
I'M NOT OKAY.

...!
UUUGH
IT'S FINE, IT'S FINE!

STOMP
STOMP
D-DID I DO SOMETHING WRONG??
NO, NO, IT'S FINE!
WE'VE HAD OTHER PEOPLE SAY NO TOO!

BANG
BANG
IT'S OKAY.
JENNY'S JUST HAVING A LIZARD BRAIN REACTION.
HIGHER FUNCTIONS KICKING IN, IN THREE, TWO, ONE—

...JENNY?

...SORRY FOR FREAKING OUT LIKE THAT!
I WAS JUST A LITTLE FRUSTRATED AT ALL THE WASTED TIME.

BUT CONSENT IS VERY IMPORTANT, SO IF YOU DON'T WANT TO...
...YOU DON'T HAVE TO.
SHAKE

TH-THANK YOU FOR YOUR TIME, JENSEN!
PUSH
NOW, YOU WON'T ***BELIEVE*** THE AMOUNT OF WORK WE HAVE TO DO...
...ARTICLES TO WRITE, VIDEOS TO EDIT...***OODLES*** OF WORK!

SO PLEASE GO AHEAD AND ENJOY THE REST OF YOUR LUNCH WHILE WE GET TO THAT.

BYE, JENSEN!
COME BY FOR LUNCH AGAIN SOMETIME!
YEAH. BYE.

KTK
...I FEEL LIKE I DID SOMETHING WRONG.

UUGH!!!
CAN YOU BELIEVE HIM?
...!
...YEP, DEFINITELY DID SOMETHING WRONG...

CAFETERIA

...THERE'S THE ART CLUB.
PEEK
...
HA HA YAMMER
...THE ONLY EMPTY SEAT IS BY TESSA...

I'M SAVING IT FOR PEPPI!
IT'S PROBABLY TAKEN...

...I'M JUST...GONNA GO O-OUTSIDE.

MAYBE I SHOULD TRY TO READ MORE OF JENNY AND AKILAH'S PAPER.
MAYBE THEN JENNY WILL BE LESS UPSET...

...WHAT IS THIS CULTURE STUFF?

"BEHAVIORAL CULTURE IS A SET OF ATTITUDES AND ACCEPTED BEHAVIOR IN A SOCIAL GROUP.
...
"IT BUILDS OVER TIME, ACTION BY ACTION, LIKE BRICK BY BRICK.
...OH, THERE'RE CARTOONS AGAIN...

"FOR EXAMPLE, EACH TIME PEOPLE THROW GARBAGE ON THE GROUND INSTEAD OF INTO A GARBAGE CAN...
"...THEY HELP BUILD A CULTURE WHERE LITTERING IS NORMALIZED AND ACCEPTED."

garbage everywhere is just how things are! everyone does it.
YEP.

...OOPS, I DO THAT.
S-SOMETIMES.

"ON THE OTHER HAND, EVERY TIME A PERSON DOESN'T LITTER, OR PICKS IT UP, OR EVEN PREVENTS IT...

"...LITTLE BY LITTLE, ACTION 'BRICK' BY ACTION 'BRICK,' THEY HELP BUILD A BEHAVIORAL CULTURE WHERE LITTERING IS *NOT* THE NORM.

"THROUGHOUT HUMAN HISTORY, EXISTING BEHAVIORAL CULTURES WERE CHALLENGED, DISMANTLED, AND NEW ONES BUILT FROM SCRATCH.

"ANYONE CAN TRY TO BUILD A CULTURE; ON A SOCIETY-WIDE SCALE, AFFECTING AN ENTIRE NATION...
"...OR EVEN ON A MUCH SMALLER SCALE, LIKE WITHIN A SINGLE FAMILY OR JUST ONE SCHOOL."
....!

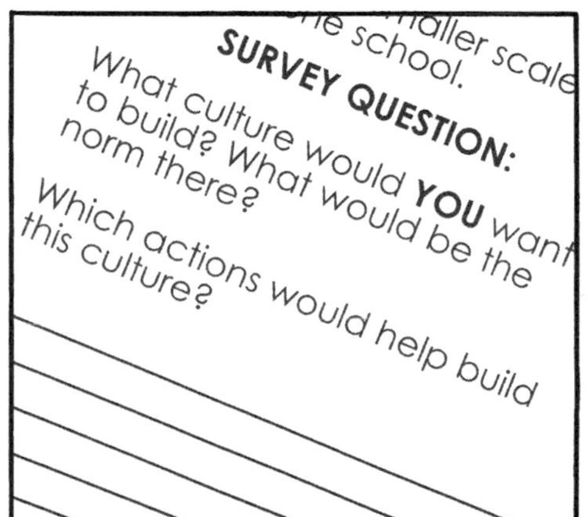
SURVEY QUESTION:
What culture would YOU want to build? What would be the norm there?
Which actions would help build this culture?

WHAT...
...CULTURE...?

...
HA HA
...
MAYBE...

...ONE...WHERE I DON'T HAVE TO...
...EAT LUNCH ALONE?

CHAPTER 7

RRING
BERRYBROOK MIDDLE SCHOOL
THE NEXT DAY.
...MY HEAD IS SWIMMING. CULTURES...? LIZARD BRAINS...?
WHY IS MIDDLE SCHOOL SO COMPLICATED...?

JENSEN, PAY ATTENTION!
IS ATTENTION A LIZARD BRAIN THING?
OR A HIGHER FUNCTION THING?

JENSEN, WAKE UP!!
I MISS JUST BEING A KID. A HUMAN ONE.

...I WONDER WHO ELSE AKILAH AND JENNY INTERVIEWED.
I WAS NUMBER TWELVE... WHO ARE THE OTHER ELEVEN?

...I BET IT WASN'T *THEM.*
HEE HEE HEE
SLINK SLINK

BTW, I *LOVE* THAT DRESS!
AWW, THANKS!
IT LOOKS JUST LIKE MY GRANDMA'S CURTAINS!

...
...SHE THREW THEM OUT RECENTLY, SAID THEY WERE TOO '80S.
...
HA HA HA HA
I'M *SO* GLAD YOU RESCUED THEM FROM THE TRASH.
...!

Shrink
WHA...?
H-ha.
Ha ha...
That's funny...
...
YOU'RE ALWAYS SUCH A JOKER, JO!

THAT...
THAT WAS LIKE WHAT TESSA AND NATHANIEL DO TO ME!

scale,
just one school.

SURVEY QUESTION:

What culture would **YOU** want to build? What would be the norm there?

Which actions would help build this culture?

PSST.
PENELOPE?
HMM?
U-UM, I'M GOING TO BE LATE FOR LUNCH, AND, UH...

C-COULD...
COULD YOU SAVE ME A SEAT?
...AT THE ART CLUB TABLE?

OH!
ACTUALLY, JAIME AND I ARE STILL WORKING ON THAT PROJECT...
...SO I WON'T BE THERE.

OH.
BUT YOU CAN ASK TESSA!

RRING
...WELL, THAT DIDN'T WORK.
WHAT ELSE CAN I DO?

...THE TABLE IS FULL AGAIN.
THERE'RE EVEN KIDS FROM THE SCIENCE CLUB?!

...
MAYBE...
...THEY'LL MAKE ROOM FOR ME?
IF I ASK...?

HA HA

...I'M AFRAID TO ASK...

LIBRARY

JENSEN!
...!
I WAS JUST ABOUT TO PING YOU!

GUESS WHAT!
THE BOOKS YOU WANTED ARE FINALLY HERE!
my badly drawn life by J.Y. Smith
INA CRUZ
fighter

....!!
WOULD YOU LIKE TO SIGN THEM OUT?
YES!

OH WOW, OH WOW.
my badly drawn life
I BETTER START WITH J.Y. SMITH—THAT'S THE ONE EVERYONE'S TALKING ABOUT.

BZZ
PING
....!

A TEXT?
...FROM PEPPI!

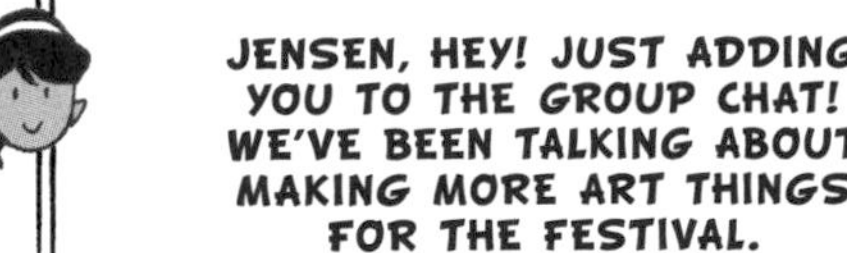
JENSEN, HEY! JUST ADDING YOU TO THE GROUP CHAT! WE'VE BEEN TALKING ABOUT MAKING MORE ART THINGS FOR THE FESTIVAL.

LOOKS LIKE TESSA FORGOT TO ADD YOU, OOPS.
(STOP DOING THAT, TESS! HA-HA!)

...SHE FORGOT TO ADD ME. AGAIN.
BZZ PING!
BZZ PING!
BZZ PING!

WHATEVER STOP BEING SO FORGETTABLE, JENSEN!

TESS, UGH.

WHAAAAT! IT'S TRUE!
every1 forgets jensen

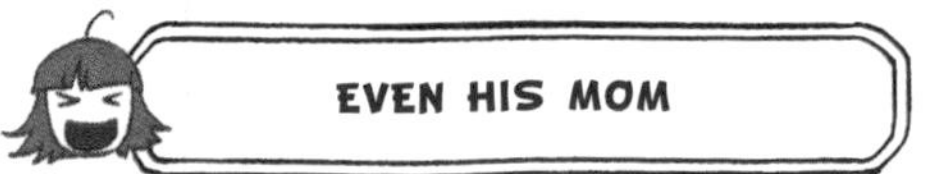
EVEN HIS MOM

BZZ PING
BZZ PING
I'M NOT...
...FORGETTABLE...

PUSH

HAPPY READING, BOOKWORM.
HA HA

...
HA HA
...IF I'M SO FORGETTABLE, WHY WON'T *THEY* FORGET ABOUT ME??

MATH TUTORING.
SIGH
...
YOU OKAY, JENSEN?

um.
...
...WHAT DO YOU THINK ABOUT THE BULLYING CULTURE AT BERRYBROOK?

....!

...Y-YEAH.
WHAT DO YOU THINK ABOUT THAT LIZARD BRAIN STUFF?
EH.

HAHA HA
DID JENNY AND AKILAH ROPE YOU INTO THEIR PROJECT TOO?
I DUNNO ABOUT THAT.
GOOD PEOPLE SOMETIMES DO BAD THINGS, AND BAD PEOPLE DO GOOD THINGS...IT'S COMPLICATED.
NOD NOD
...I LIKE THE STUFF ABOUT CHANGING CULTURE THOUGH.
FIXING WHAT DOESN'T WORK...

...I'D BE GAME FOR THAT.
...

...AARON'S SO SMART.
HIM AND VICKIE BOTH.
(TURNS OUT SHE'S HERE BECAUSE THEY'RE PRACTICING FOR A MATH COMPETITION!!)

...ME, I STILL CAN'T DO MY MATH HOMEWORK WITHOUT HELP...
...OR READ THAT LIZARD BRAIN PAPER.

WHAT IF...
WHAT IF I **AM** STUPID? LIKE PEOPLE SAY?

MAYBE I SHOULDN'T EVEN TRY...
...TO BE A NASA ASTRONAUT...

THE NEXT DAY.

HA
HA
HA

SHOVE
HA HA

HE'S SO FAT, HE CAN'T EVEN FIT, HA-HA!
HA
...

HA HA
...

LUNCH.
HA HA HA
THE TABLE IS FULL AGAIN.

my badly drawn life
by J.Y. Smith
...WHY DO PEOPLE LIKE THIS BOOK...?

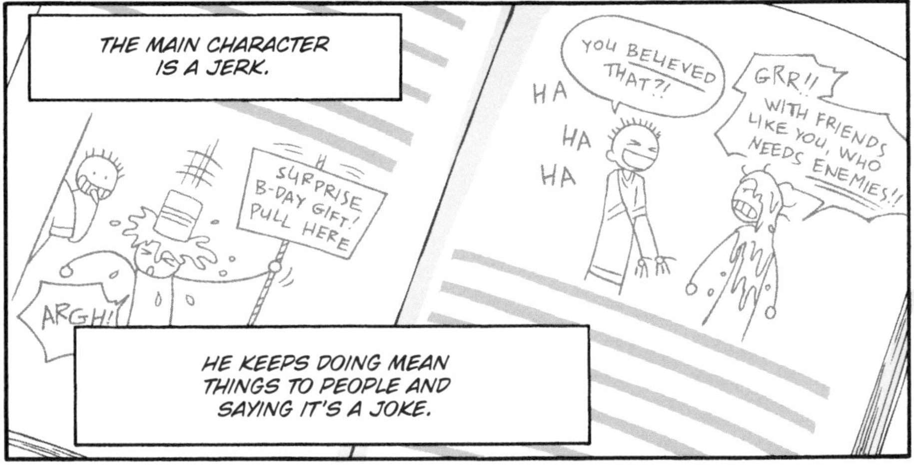
THE MAIN CHARACTER IS A JERK.
SURPRISE B-DAY GIFT! PULL HERE
ARGH!
HA HA HA
YOU BELIEVED THAT?!
GRR!! WITH FRIENDS LIKE YOU, WHO NEEDS ENEMIES!!
HE KEEPS DOING MEAN THINGS TO PEOPLE AND SAYING IT'S A JOKE.

"WITH FRIENDS LIKE YOU, WHO NEEDS ENEMIES!!"

...

THE NEXT DAY.
I WILL NOW RETURN YOUR QUIZ RESULTS!

JENSEN.

ONLY A "D"...?
I THOUGHT I'D DO BETTER, AFTER TUTORING...

...
...SO MUCH FOR BEING A NASA ASTRONAUT.

RRING
LUNCH.

...I SHOULD CHECK WITH THE NEWSPAPER. MAYBE THEY NEED HELP!

JENSEN!
UH...
NOW'S ACTUALLY NOT A GOOD TIME...

WE'RE SWAMPED. SORRY...
AKILAH, ARE YOU DONE DRAF—
MY DRAMA CLUB ARTICLE GOT PULLED! SO NOW, WE HAVE TO FILL A CONTENT HOLE...

...AND NO ONE'S SUBMITTED ANYTHING FOR THE SUBMISSIONS CALL...
O-OH.
GOOD LUCK!
THANKS, JENSEN!

BYE!
KTK

...JENNY HASN'T TEXTED ME IN SEVERAL DAYS...SHE'S EITHER STILL MAD AT ME...
CAFETERIA
...OR THEY DON'T NEED ME.

...
...DOES ANYONE NEED ME?

...

RRSTLE

BRR
...IT'S COLD TODAY.

...SHOULD I...
...WORK ON SOMETHING...?

...MY ZOMBIE PLAN?
IF ZOMBIES COME...
...I COULD...
RARG
RAWR
...
...HIDE?
OR I COULD JUST...
...STAND THERE...
RAWR
RARG
...AND LET THEM... EAT ME...

RRING
ALL RIGHT, TEN PUSHUPS AND TEN JUMPING JACKS.

cough
cough
EEW, JENSEN, STOP SPREADING YOUR GERMS!
HA HA
EVACUATE THE AREA!

JENSEN, ARE YOU OKAY?
YOU DON'T LOOK SO GOOD.

COUGH
MBLL
WOBBLE
...RIGHT. HOW ABOUT WE GET YOU TO THE NURSE'S OFFICE?
GUIDANCE/ NURSE

OH YEAH, YOU'RE DEFINITELY BURNING UP.

LOOKS LIKE IT'S A FLU. I'M GOING TO RECOMMEND THAT YOU STAY HOME FOR A FEW DAYS.
SHIVER

I'LL BE CALLING YOUR MOTHER TO COME GET YOU.
IS THERE A FRIEND YOU WANT TO PICK UP YOUR HOMEWORK WHILE YOU'RE OUT SICK?
...

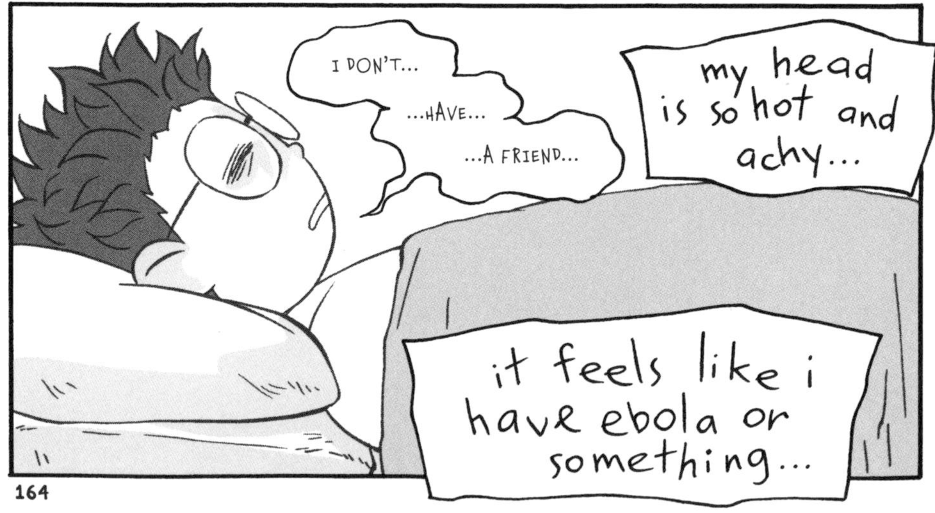
I DON'T...
...HAVE...
...A FRIEND...
my head is so hot and achy...
it feels like i have ebola or something...

maybe it's some new unknown disease...
and i'll have to be quarantined...
STUDY HIM BUT CAREFULLY.
WE CAN'T RISK EXPOSURE TO THE REST OF HUMANITY.
...and spend the rest of my life in isolation...
i'd do it.
to save everyone.
at least then i'd be of some use.

CHAPTER 8

A WEEK LATER.

...IT WAS JUST A FLU, AFTER ALL...
BERRYBROOK MIDDLE SCHOOL
...OR SO THE DOCTOR CLAIMS.
I TRIED TO GET THEM TO RUN MORE TESTS, BUT...

...THEY SAID IT'S TIME TO GO BACK.
(SO IF I START A ZOMBIE EPIDEMIC, IT'LL BE THEIR FAULT.)

RRING
EVERYTHING IS THE SAME. IT'S LIKE I NEVER LEFT...

...EXCEPT I MISSED THE ARTS FESTIVAL.

...I LOST FOUR POUNDS WHILE SICK THOUGH.
MAYBE NOW PEOPLE WON'T CALL ME FAT?

SHOVE
FATSO, YOU'RE BACK!

...OR NOT.
HA HA HA HA HA

HAVE YOU GUYS SEEN FELICITY?
IS SHE BACK?
I DON'T THINK SO...
...?

FELICITY?
ART CLUB FELICITY?

...!
JUSTICE 4 FELICITY!!
BRING HER BACK!!!
...IT IS HER!
WHAAA...

...WHAT DID I MISS NOW?
JUSTICE 4 FELICITY!!
BRING HER BACK!!!
RRRAANG
ENGLISH.
JENSEN!

YOU'RE BACK!
ARE YOU FEELING BETTER?
U-UH, YEAH, A LOT BETTER!
THANKS.

WHAT'S THAT ABOUT FELICITY?
I SAW THE FLYERS.
UGH, IT'S SO UNFAIR WHAT THEY DID, JENSEN!!

WH-WHAT HAPPENED?
SO, REMEMBER SHE WAS GOING TO DRESS UP FOR THE ARTS FESTIVAL?
AS SAILOR SUNBURST, THAT ANIME CHARACTER?

WELL, SHE *DID*, AND SHE LOOKED ***AMAZING***.
HER SISTER RIGGED UP THESE FANS WITH FABRIC STRIPS FOR SPECIAL EFFECTS...
...AND SHE HAD RIBBONS—SHE LOOKED LIKE A PRO, JENSEN. I'M NOT EVEN KIDDING.
...BUT THEN, SUDDENLY, THE SCHOOL ADMIN RUNS OVER—
WHAT DO YOU THINK YOU'RE WEARING, YOUNG LADY?!
GO CHANGE IMMEDIATELY!
HUH? WHA...?
THAT SKIRT BARELY EXISTS! COVER UP THOSE LEGS! THIS IS A SCHOOL, NOT A NIGHTCLUB!

...!
YOU CAN'T MAKE ME DO THAT!
SHE REFUSED TO CHANGE.
SO THEY SAID SHE VIOLATED THE DRESS CODE RULES...
....!
...AND SUSPENDED HER!
...BECAUSE OF HER SKIRT?
NO.
BECAUSE THE SCHOOL RULES ARE STUPID.
STOMP STOMP
HOLD THAT THOUGHT, JORGE.
....!
SLAM
TAK TAK TAK
CLASS, NO PRESENTATION WORK TODAY.
I KNOW EVERYONE WANTS TO TALK ABOUT THE CURRENT EVENTS, SO LET'S MAKE IT A CLASS DISCUSSION.

...JORGE, PLEASE START BY EXPLAINING YOUR COMMENT ON MISS TEALE'S SUSPENSION.

...UH, I DON'T MEAN TO BE DISRESPECTFUL, MISS LEE, BUT...THEY'RE MAKING HER MISS *CLASSES*...
...OVER A *SKIRT.*
WOW, I'VE NEVER SEEN MISS LEE SO ANGRY.

TRUE. THE SCHOOL ADMIN DECIDED THAT A GIRL'S *CLOTHES* WERE MORE IMPORTANT THAN HER *EDUCATION*.
CLASS, WHAT ARE YOUR THOUGHTS ON THIS?

WELL, SHE DID BREAK THE RULES, MISS LEE.
SHE SHOULD'VE WORN A LONGER SKIRT.
ALSO TRUE. SHE COULD'VE WORN A LONGER SKIRT.
HOW LONG A SKIRT, DO YOU THINK?
...
I DUNNO.
LIKE, KNEE-LENGTH?

...AND DO YOU THINK IT'S FAIR THAT *YOU* SHOULD DECIDE THE LENGTH OF *HER* SKIRT?
uh.
WHAT ABOUT IF *SHE* DECIDED THE LENGTH OF *YOURS*?
...
. . .
...ALL RIGHT, LET'S CONSIDER SOME HISTORY HERE. I SEE A NUMBER OF GIRLS ARE WEARING PANTS.
THIS USED TO BE FROWNED UPON. IN 1938, HELEN HULICK WAS *JAILED* FOR WEARING SLACKS— PUT BEHIND BARS.
CLASS, WHAT ARE YOUR THOUGHTS ON *THAT*?
DO YOU THINK SOCIETY SHOULD HAVE THE RIGHT TO JAIL OR PUNISH YOU FOR WHAT YOU CHOOSE TO WEAR?

...

EVOLUTION OF CIVIL LIBERTIES: THEN AND NOW.
SKRT
ALL RIGHT, I WANT EVERYONE TO WRITE DOWN SOME DISCUSSION POINTS AND THEN BREAK UP INTO GROUPS.

RRRING
YAMMER
WOW, MISS LEE WAS INTENSE TODAY.

YEAH. I DIDN'T KNOW ABOUT ALL THAT STUFF.
...THAT DOESN'T HELP US GET FELICITY BACK THOUGH!
WE'VE ***GOT*** TO COME UP WITH SOME WAY.

ART CLUB IS MEETING OUTSIDE FOR LUNCH TODAY—WE'RE GONNA BRAINSTORM IDEAS AGAIN.
ARE YOU COMING? WANT ME TO SAVE YOU A SPOT?

Y-YES!
YES, PLEASE!
GREAT, I'LL SEE YOU THERE!

WOW.
...PEPPI'S REALLY NICE.

JUSTICE 4 FELICITY!!
BRING HER BACK!!!
...

...WAIT.
I THINK I KNOW WHO CAN HELP!

RRING
LUNCH.
THE NEWSPAPER CREW! THEY'RE THE JUSTICE SQUAD! THEY'RE ALL ABOUT THIS STUFF!

HEEEY, SPACEMAN!
FELIPE!
ARE JENNY AND AKILAH HERE?
I HAVE TO TELL THEM—
UH.
MAAAYBE NOT A GOOD TIME?

W-WOW... WHAT'S WRONG?
TAK
TAK
TAK
...

TURN
WHAT DO YOU WANT, JENSEN?

U-UH...
FELICITY... SUSPENDED... ...HELP...?
OH, DON'T ASK ***HER*** FOR HELP, JENSEN.

I'VE BEEN OVER THIS WITH MISS OH-NO ALREADY.
UGH, NOT THIS AGAIN.
SHE'D RATHER SWEEP IT UNDER A ***RUG*** THAN ***REPORT*** ON IT.

LOOK.
EVEN IF WE WROTE THE ARTICLE, THEY WOULD NEVER LET US PUBLISH IT!

YOU DON'T KNOW THAT! NOT IF YOU DON'T EVEN TRY!
I DO KNOW THAT! I KNOW EXACTLY WHAT'LL HAPPEN!!
THE SAME THING THAT HAPPENED WITH YOUR STUPID DRAMA CLUB ARTICLE!

...MY "STUPID"...?!
RRSTL
WE SPENT ALL THAT TIME! ENERGY! AND WHAT DID THEY SAY?!

"THIS MATTER IS BEST HANDLED AS AN INTERNAL INVESTIGATION. PLEASE FOLLOW SCHOOL RULES, OR YOUR CLUB WILL BE SUSPENDED."

SUSPENDED, AKILAH!
THEY COULD SHUT DOWN THE NEWSPAPER!
THEY ALREADY ***HAVE***!!
THEY KEEP SHUTTING DOWN ALL THE ***REAL STORIES***!!

DO YOU WANT TO KEEP WRITING USELESS ARTICLES AND HALLWAY GOSSIP?

USELESS?! SOME PEOPLE LIKE READING HALLWAY GOSSIP! NOT EVERYONE'S A SNOBBY ELITE JOURNALIST WANNABE!
AND IF YOU'D JUST STOP BEING STUPID AND STUBBORN ABOUT—
.....!!

...Y-YOU KNOW WHAT?
HOW ABOUT I STOP BEING HERE, *PERIOD.*

IF YOU WANT TO KEEP RUNNING USELESS CRAP, YOU *DO* THAT.
....!
I QUIT.

. . .
...
o-oh yeah?

well...
well, FINE!

...i
I DON'T NEED YOU!
I DON'T NEED ANY OF YOU!!!
EVERYONE, GET OUT!!
D-DON'T COME BACK!!

SLAM
WH-WHAT JUST HAPPENED?
WAS THAT A FRIEND-FIGHT...?
NOOOPE.
THAT WAS A REAL FIGHT.

...I'M JUST...
...GONNA GO. AND NOT COME BACK FOR A WHILE.
...

CAFETERIA

JENSEN, THERE YOU ARE!

PEPPI DID SAVE ME A SEAT!
OVER HERE, COME SIT!
OKAY, SO HERE'S THE IDEA LIST SO FAR—

CHEW
CHEW
FLIP
FLIP

...

...JENSEN!
HUH?
DO *YOU* HAVE ANY IDEAS?
U-UH...
I'M THINKING...?

...WELL, HOW ABOUT PUTTING UP MORE FLYERS?
THAT DID *NOTHING*!
...
CAN WE DO A FUND-RAISER?
FOR *WHAT*?

...IF EVEN THE NEWSPAPER CAN'T HELP...

...WHAT CAN ANYONE DO?

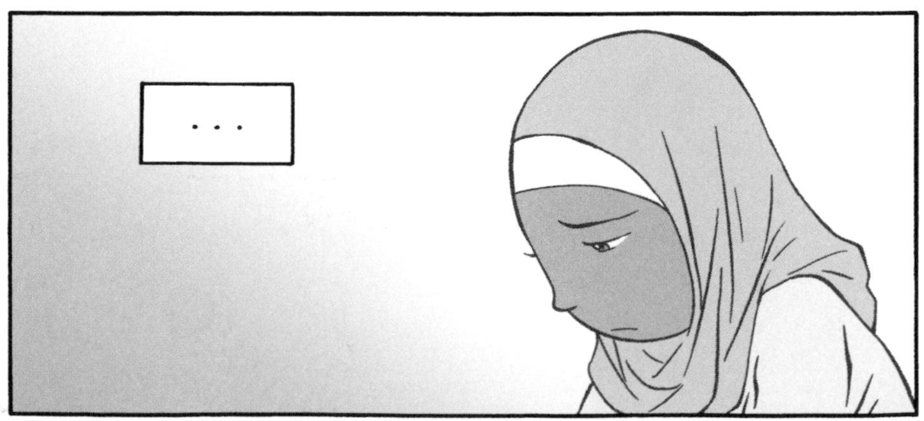
...

CHAPTER 9

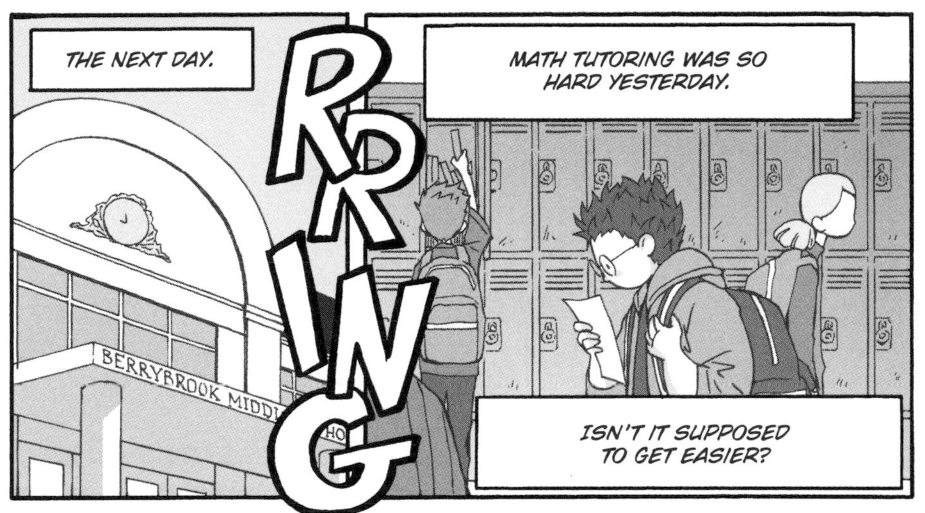
THE NEXT DAY.
RRING
MATH TUTORING WAS SO HARD YESTERDAY.
BERRYBROOK MIDDL
ISN'T IT SUPPOSED TO GET EASIER?

JUSTICE 4 FELICITY!!
BRING HER BACK!!!
...
...FELICITY'S STILL NOT BACK...

...

...AND THE NEWSPAPER CREW IS STILL BROKEN.

MATH.
SIGH...
RRRING
ALL RIGHT, CLASS DISMISSED!
AS YOU LEAVE, PICK UP THESE PRACTICE PROBLEMS FOR NEXT WEEK'S TEST!

JENSEN.
Y-YES?
AARON TELLS ME YOU ARE MAKING PROGRESS IN TUTORING.
GOOD JOB.
....!
R-REALLY?
BUT...
...I STILL DON'T UNDERSTAND EVEN HALF OF IT...

YOU'RE JUST VERY BEHIND, JENSEN. THAT'S ALL.
IT'LL TAKE TIME AND HARD WORK, BUT YOU'LL CATCH UP.
JUST KEEP GOING AND DON'T QUIT.

...HUH.
MAYBE HE'S NOT THAT EVIL, AFTER ALL.

CAFETERIA

...I HOPE THERE'S A SPOT AT THE ART TABLE. BET THEY'RE STILL TRYING TO HELP FELICITY...

...I STILL DON'T HAVE A SINGLE IDEA FOR THAT.

...!
FOSTER AND YANIC!!

...PHEW, THEY DIDN'T SEE ME.
HA
HA
...BETTER KEEP IT THAT WAY.

...I THINK I'LL JUST
EAT OUTSIDE.

I CAN BRAINSTORM
SOME IDEAS ON HOW TO
HELP FELICITY!

...

...AKILAH.

...SH-SHOULD I MAKE
SURE SHE'S OKAY?
OR DOES SHE WANT
TO BE LEFT ALONE...?

...I-I'LL ASK.
IF SHE WANTS ME TO LEAVE, I WILL.

H-HI, AKILAH!
...
IS THIS SPOT TAKEN?

...
UM... NO.

...

...H-HOW ARE YOU?
...!

...
FINE.

SHE DOESN'T LOOK FINE.
...I'M NO GOOD AT THIS... I DON'T KNOW WHAT TO SAY.

U-UH.
IT'S SURE WEIRD TO SEE YOU WITHOUT JENNY.

...OOPS. SHOULD I HAVE SAID THAT?! I DON'T—
...
IT IS WEIRD.

WE'VE ALWAYS HUNG OUT TOGETHER.
SINCE KINDERGARTEN!

WOW, YOU MET IN KINDERGARTEN?
...
YEAH. WE WERE, LIKE, FIVE?

THESE TWO BIGGER KIDS WERE HARASSING ME...

...AND JENNY CAME RIGHT OVER...
...AND TOLD THEM TO GO COUNT ALL THE CRAYONS FOR THEIR MISBEHAVIOR.
SHE ACTUALLY SAID THAT WORD, "MISBEHAVIOR."
uh, one, two, four
THEY WENT AND DID IT TOO—
SHE WAS SO IMPOSING AND SURE OF HER RIGHTNESS.
SHE WAS *FIVE*.
. . .
...SHE *ALWAYS* THINKS SHE'S THE ONE WHO'S RIGHT.

SNFFLE
....!

A-ARE...
...ARE YOU OKAY?

NO!
I MISS MY BEST FRIEND!
I HATE THAT WE HAD THAT HUGE FIGHT!

....!
...
M-MAYBE YOU'LL MAKE UP?
MAYBE IT'S JUST...
...LIZARD BRAIN STUFF?
....!
...WHAT?!
THAT HAS NOTHING TO DO WITH—

...

...WAIT.
...WE WERE ANGRY. AND HURT.
...SO WE LASHED OUT...
...INSTEAD OF PROBLEM SOLVING.

...IT TOTALLY ***WAS***.
IT WAS A LIZARD BRAIN REACTION.

...

C'MON, JENSEN!!
...?
IT'S NOT TOO LATE TO FIX THIS!

NEWSPAPER
OFFICE

JENNY?
WE GOTTA TALK!

Akilah?
Wha—
What do you want?

NEWSPAPER OFFICE
...JENNY...
...ARE YOU CRYING?
NO!!
WHY ARE YOU GUYS HERE?!!

I...
I CAME TO APOLOGIZE...
...FOR... FOR JUST WALKING OUT LIKE THAT...
...FOR SAYING THE STUFF I SAID.

...!
...I'M SORRY.
DO YOU WANNA BE FRIENDS AGAIN?

OH MY GOD, I'M THE ONE WHO'S SORRY!!
I SAID TERRIBLE STUFF TO YOU!!

I'M SO GLAD YOU'RE BACK!!
I PROMISE I WON'T BE A JERK ANYMORE!!

FRIENDS AGAIN?
TO THE END OF THE WORLD!
POKE
HEEEY.
IS IT SAFE TO COME BACK?

...OH GOOD, YOU GUYS ALL MADE UP.
LISTEN, WE *REALLY* GOTTA FIGURE SOMETHING OUT FOR FELICITY. IT'S NOT FAIR.

YES!!
WE'RE BACK, AND WE'RE GONNA DO THIS!!

I'VE BEEN RACKING MY BRAIN ON THIS... WHAT CAN WE EVEN DO?
WE CAN'T PUT ANYTHING IN THE PAPER...
CAN WE TRY TO SNEAK IT INTO BERRY SCOOP?
...NOOOO, THAT'S MONITORED BY THE SCHOOL ADMIN TOO.
SNORE

...I WAS THINKING— WHAT IF WE START A PETITION?
GET STUDENTS AND TEACHERS TO SIGN IT, THEN TAKE IT TO THE SCHOOL BOARD?
THEY MIGHT TAKE THAT MORE SERIOUSLY.
...!

OMG YES
THAT'S EXACTLY WHAT WE WILL DO!!
...WE HAVE A PLAN?

THE NEXT DAY.
ALL RIGHT, EVERYONE, HERE IT IS, FRESH OFF THE PRINTER!
PETITION: BRING BACK FELICITY!!!
ADD YOUR NAME TO JOIN THE RIGHT SIDE OF HISTORY!
WE ARE PETITIONING TO:
*LIFT FELICITY'S SUSPENSION!!
*UPDATE THE SCHOOL DRESS CODE FROM THE 18TH CENTURY TO THE 21ST!!
name class
name class
11
12
13
14
BERRYBROO

ART CLUB!
SCIENCE CLUB!
EVERYONE ELSE!
WE NEED **ONE HUNDRED** SIGNATURES...
...BY THE END OF **TODAY!**
WE HAVE A PLAN!

SO, EACH ONE OF YOU—TAKE A SHEET AND GET AS MANY SIGNATURES AS YOU CAN BY THE LAST BELL!
BRING THEM BACK HERE, AND WE'LL COLLECT THEM FOR THE MEETING.
DO **NOT** BE LATE!

RRING

...I GOTTA GET LOTS OF SIGNATURES.
...H-HOW ARE WE SUPPOSED TO DO THIS?

DO YOU THINK IT'S FAIR THAT YOU CAN GET SUSPENDED OVER A *SKIRT*?
WHAT?! **NO!**
THEN YOU SHOULD SIGN OUR PETITION!

OHHH.

...DO YOU THINK IT'S FAIR THAT—
UH.
PASS.
O-OKAY.

...WOULD YOU LIKE TO SIGN—
UGH, WHAT? LEAVE ME ALONE.

OOOKAY...THIS IS HARDER THAN IT LOOKED.

HEY!
HEY, YOU!
WEIRD GUY! YES, YOU!
COME OVER HERE!

IS THAT THE PETITION?
U-UH, YES...
GIMME.
SNATCH
WH-WHAT IS SHE GONNA...?

YOU'RE SIGNING IT?
YES! AND YOU SHOULD TOO!
SCRIBBLL
THE DRESS RULES ARE STUPID— LIZ GOT IN TROUBLE FOR LEGGINGS!

THEY'D MAKE US WEAR POTATO SACKS IF THEY COULD!
HERE, GUY.
SHOVE
LET'S GO.

...!
...I GOT MY FIRST SIGNATURE!

SEVERAL HOURS LATER.
THIS IS EXHAUSTING...
I'VE ASKED SO MANY PEOPLE...

...BUT ONLY GOT THREE SIGNATURES.
I HOPE OTHERS ARE HAVING BETTER LUCK.

GAH!
SNATCH
HEY, FATSO, WHATCHA GOT THERE?

OH, LOOK, IT'S A PETIIIIITION!
H-HEY
WITH ONLY THREE PEOPLE WHO CARE!
HA
HA

H-HEY!!!
....!
P-PLEASE GIVE THAT BACK!

I NEED THAT!
CRMPLE
PWEESE GIVE THAT BACK, WEH-WEH-WEH!

OH, WHOOPS!
IT'S GARBAGE NOW!

HAHAHA
....!

UGH!!

...WE NEED THOSE SIGNATURES!
rummage
rummage

WHY'S HE DIGGING IN THE TRASH?
EEW, GROSS.
THIS IS SO EMBARRASSING...
MUST... FIND...FOR FELICITY...
GOT IT!!

...JENSEN?
HEY, BUDDY, IS EVERYTHING OKAY?
JORGE!
OLIVIA!
...D-DO YOU GUYS WANT TO SIGN OUR PETITION?

RRING
DASH
...JORGE AND OLIVIA DIDN'T JUST SIGN THE PETITION...
...THEY GOT THEIR ENTIRE ATHLETICS CLUB TO SIGN IT TOO!!
I'VE GOT TWENTY-SIX SIGNATURES!!

HERE THEY ARE!
JENSEN!! FINALLY!
YOU'RE THE LAST ONE!

...WHY'S IT ALL CRUMPLED?
...OH, WOW, TWENTY-SIX?! NOW WE DEFINITELY HAVE ENOUGH!!

IS EVERYONE READY TO GO HERE?
WE NEED TO CATCH THE PRINCIPAL BEFORE HE LEAVES.
MISS LEE!

HE WON'T LEAVE. I TOLD PHIL TO HOLD HIM AS LONG AS IT TAKES.
WE'RE GETTING THIS BALL ROLLING TODAY.
AGREED.
...!
AND MISS TOBINS! AND MR. KRISTOFFER?!!

...EVEN THE TEACHERS ARE GETTING INVOLVED?!
WE HAVE ALL THE SIGNATURES! READY TO ROLL!
GREAT, LET'S GO!

...DOES THAT MEAN ME TOO?

....!
JENSEN?
WHY AREN'T YOU AT TUTORING?
....!

OR NOT.
IS THIS ENOUGH? 112 SIGNATURES, THAT'S TONS.

TUTORING.
CLICK
CLICK
CLICK
...I'M ON PINS AND NEEDLES.
WILL THEY GET FELICITY BACK?!

HEY!
STOP CLICKING THAT PEN! IT'S **ANNOYING**.

...OH YEAH, YANIC IS HERE AGAIN.
...
...ARE YOU NERVOUS ABOUT YOUR LITTLE PETITION THAT NO ONE CARES ABOUT?

...
BET THEY'RE BEING TOLD TO TAKE A HIKE **RIGHT NOW**.
...
HA!

...IS IT JUST ME, OR IS YANIC GETTING WORSE...?
I MEAN, HE WAS NEVER AWESOME...
...BUT IT'S LIKE HE'S EXTRA EVIL LATELY.

MUST...NOT...
...LET HIM GET TO ME...
HA
H
HA

CHAPTER 10

THE NEXT DAY.
RRING
HOMEROOM.
BERRYBROOK MIDDLE
H-HOW DID IT GO YESTERDAY?
UH... GOOD?
I THINK?

...THE PRINCIPAL SAID THEY WILL "REVIEW" IT IN A "TIMELY MANNER"!
WHATEVER THAT MEANS.
I THOUGHT FELICITY WOULD BE BACK BY NOW.

RRSTLE BEEP

ATTENTION, STUDENTS.
THIS IS YOUR PRINCIPAL SPEAKING.

I WOULD LIKE TO START BY COMMENDING YOUR PASSION ON BEHALF OF YOUR FELLOW STUDENT, FELICITY TEALE.
THE SCHOOL BOARD HAS RECEIVED YOUR PETITION AND IS CONSIDERING IT VERY CAREFULLY.
AS A RESULT, WE WILL BE TAKING THE SCHOOL DRESS CODE UNDER IMMEDIATE REVIEW, AND WE ASK FOR YOUR FEEDBACK ON UPDATING AND IMPROVING IT TO BE FAIR TO EVERYONE.
YOUR TEACHERS WILL HAVE A QUESTIONNAIRE FORM — PLEASE FILL ONE OUT AND HAND IT IN BEFORE THE END OF TODAY.
THANK YOU FOR YOUR EFFORTS IN HELPING RESOLVE THIS ISSUE.
GOOD DAY.

CLICK
...

...THAT'S IT?
WHAT ABOUT FELICITY?

I GUESS THEY...WANT TO UPDATE THE DRESS CODE... FIRST?
UGH.
I'M JUST GOING TO WRITE "BRING BACK FELICITY" ALL OVER THEIR STUPID QUESTIONNAIRE.

BZZ
PING!

...A TEXT?
BZZ
...?
BZZ
HEY, I GOT A TEXT.

...FROM FELICITY!
IT'S TO THE WHOLE GROUP.

!
GUYS GUYS WHAAAAT
THEY JUST CALLED MY MOM
...SHE'S STILL TYPING.

...!

...THEY LIFTED THE SUSPENSION?!
YUS!!
WHAT?!
OMG!!

IT DID WORK!!
IT WORKED!!
SHE'S BACK!!!
AAAAAA

...IT WORKED!

...I CAN'T BELIEVE YOU GUYS DID THAT WHOLE PETITION THING FOR ME!

HOW DID YOU EVEN...?

BELIEVE IT, LADY!

WE WENT ALL OVER THE WHOLE SCHOOL!

T-TWENTY-SIX.
TWENTY-SIX ???!

AWW, C'MERE.
BEAR HUG
THANKS, BUDDY.

MAN, IT'S GOOD TO BE BACK. SO WHAT DID I MISS?
AUGH, SO MUCH DRAMA. HA-HA!
...I'VE NEVER GOTTEN HUGGED BEFORE.
(EXCEPT FROM FAMILY)

I GUESS MIDDLE SCHOOL LIFE CAN BE GOOD, AFTER ALL.

RRING
BERRYBROOK MIDDLE SC
FELICITY BEING BACK WAS HUGE NEWS THAT ENTIRE WEEK.

THE DRESS CODE UPDATE TOO...BIG DRAMA.
A FIVE-INCH SKIRT IS NOT A SKIRT! IT'S A BELT!!
WHY ARE YOU SUCH A PRUDE?!

AKILAH AND JENNY LOVED IT.
BICKER
ARGUE
AHHH, THE SWEET, SWEET SOUND OF DEMOCRACY AT WORK...

WE ARE COLLECTING FEEDBACK TO FEATURE ON BERRY SCOOP—WOULD YOU GUYS LIKE TO COMMENT ON RECORD?
fight! fight!
WOULD I?!!
ME TOO!!

...BUT THEN, OLIVIA BROKE UP WITH SEAN, RIGHT IN THE MIDDLE OF THE CAFETERIA.
L-LIV, C'MON, HE'S NOT WORTH IT.
I SAW YOUR TEXTS TO MICHELLE, YOU JERK!!!
COME OVER HERE AND FIGHT ME!!!
DUDE, RUN.
RUN NOW.
OLIVIA TAKES JIUJITSU AND KARATE.

...EVERYONE WAS VERY SURPRISED BECAUSE WE ALL THOUGHT SHE WAS DATING JORGE.
did you hear?!
omg i was so surprised!!

...AND THEN, END-OF-THE-YEAR PROJECT DUE DATES AND TESTS CAME...
FIFTY PROBLEMS BY THE END OF THE WEEK!

...AND EVERYONE BECAME TOO BUSY TRYING NOT TO FAIL TO GOSSIP ABOUT ANYTHING.
GROAN
UUUGH
WHYEEe

SO NOW, EVERYTHING IS PRETTY MUCH BACK TO NORMAL...

...INCLUDING...
GLANCE
LOOK

....!
THERE HE IS!

ACTUALLY, FOSTER AND YANIC DIDN'T JUST GET BACK TO NORMAL...
DASH
...THEY GOT **WORSE.**
DID I LOSE THEM?
I USED TO BE ABLE TO AVOID THEM, BUT NOW...
...IT'S LIKE THEY'RE EVERYWHERE.

IN THE CAFETERIA...
HA HA
HA
hey, look, i'm jensen!
HA HA HA
HA

IN THE HALLWAYS BETWEEN CLASSES...
THEY'RE AT MY LOCKER AGAIN!

SOMETIMES EVEN AFTER MATH TUTORING!
...!

U-UM, C-CAN I WALK WITH YOU GUYS?
UH.
SURE.

AND THEY'RE REALLY SNEAKY.
THEY NEVER DO IT IN FRONT OF ADULTS, OR EVEN JORGE AND OLIVIA...
'SUP, JENSEN.
H-HI.

...
fat and stupid
...SO I CAN'T PROVE ANYTHING.

...I DON'T KNOW WHAT TO DO.

NEWSPAPER OFFICE.
....!!
....!!
YOU SHOULD REPORT THEM, JENSEN!!!
IT'S OBVIOUS THEY'RE TARGETING YOU!!!

TELL A TEACHER! A SCHOOL COUNSELOR! ANY ADULT!!

ISN'T...ISN'T THAT SNITCHING?

...WHAT?! NO!!

IT'S SELF-DEFENSE! THEY'RE POISONING YOUR LIFE!

IT'S LIKE— IF THERE WERE TWO ***VENOMOUS SNAKES*** AFTER YOU, YOU NEED TO REPORT THEM TO PEST CONTROL!

IT'S KINDA DANGEROUS...
...BECAUSE I'M NOT SURE IT'LL EVEN WORK ON THEM, BUT...
...DO YOU WANNA HEAR IT?

THE NEXT DAY.

RRING
BROOK MIDDLE SCHOOL

MATH TUTORING.
OKAY, I THINK THAT'S IT FOR TODAY.
DO YOU HAVE ANY MORE QUESTIONS, JENSEN?

U-UH, NO.
I THINK I GET IT.

YOU'RE GETTING A LOT BETTER, JENSEN!
....!
THANKS, VICKIE.

DID YOU WANT TO WALK WITH US AGAIN?
...

UM.
...TH-THANKS, BUT I GOTTA GET SOMETHING FROM MY LOCKER.

...I DON'T REALLY HAVE TO GET ANYTHING FROM MY LOCKER.

I'M GOING TO...
...DO THE THING...
...AKILAH TOLD ME ABOUT.

...I'VE NEVER BEEN SO SCARED IN MY LIFE.

RRSTLE
KTK

PEEK

I DON'T SEE THEM...
...ANYWHERE...

MAYBE...
...THEY ALREADY WENT HOME?
KTK
THEN I WOULDN'T...HAVE TO DO THIS.

HEY LOOK, THERE HE IS!
...
CRAP.

I WAS STARTING TO THINK YOU WERE AVOIDING US, JENSEN!
I WAS **HURT**!
HE WAS **SO** HURT.

OH GOD.
STAY CALM, STAY CALM.
...
...
HOW'D TUTORING GO?
YOU STILL DUMB AS A BAG OF ROCKS?

D-DON'T PANIC...
YOU CAN DO THIS.
...IS IT ME, OR IS HE EVEN FATTER TODAY?
...
...
MUST BE THAT BURGER HE HAD FOR LUNCH, HA-HA!

J-JUST LIKE AKILAH MADE ME PRACTICE...
BU-BUMP
...
BU-BUMP
HHUH
HUH

HEY, FATSO, **SAY** SOMETHING.
JUST...JUST TELL THEM—
BU-BUMP

P-P—
PLEASE STOP...
...DOING THIS.

...
...HUH?

...
P-PLEASE STOP CALLING ME NAMES...
...AND...AND MAKING FUN OF ME.
IT'S...IT'S ***HARASSMENT***, AND IT'S MAKING MY LIFE ***HELL***...

YOU'RE...
YOU'RE REALLY HURTING ME.
PLEASE STOP.

SNERK
ARE YOU FOR *REAL*?
. . .

CAN YOU *BELIEVE* THIS WIMP?
WEH-WEH-WEH, MY LIFE IS HELL. PWEEZE STAAAHP.
. . .

HA HA
REALAAAX!
WE'RE JUST HAVING FUN WITH YOU!
IT'S...
IT'S NOT FUN FOR *ME*!

WELL, THEN LIGHTEN UP!
YOINK

....!
H-HEY!
GIVE THEM BACK!
I NEED THEM!
D'URR, LOOK AT ME. I'M JENSEN!
WEH-WEH. I NEED THEM!
UH...
H-HEY, LET'S JUST GO, MAN.
GIVE THEM BACK.

WHAAAT? IT'S FUNNY!
JUST... JUST GIVE THEM BACK.

...
WHAT'S YOUR DEAL?
I JUST WANNA GO, OKAY?
GIVE HIM BACK HIS STUFF.

FINE.
SCOFF
TOSS
FETCH, FOUR-EYES.

KTK

CLINK

NO!
DUDE, YOU BROKE THEM!!
...!
N-NO, I DIDN'T!
THEY MUST'VE BEEN ALREADY BROKEN!
ENOUGH.

YANIC, WHAT IS EVEN WRONG WITH YOU?!
....!!
JENSEN, ARE YOU OKAY?!
...!
WERE YOU RECORDING?!
I'M STILL RECORDING, YOU TROGLODYTE! WE ALL ARE!
SAY HELLO TO THE SCHOOL BOARD THAT'S GONNA SEE THIS!
DASH
WH-WHAT ARE YOU GUYS DOING HERE?
YOU CAN'T DO THAT!
WE WERE TAILING THEM, TRYING TO GET BULLYING PROOF...
JENSEN, YOUR GLASSES...I'M SO SORRY.

YOU ERASE THAT VIDEO, OR I'LL—
HEY, WHAT'S ALL THIS YELLING?

WHAT'S GOING ON HERE?

u-uh.

...YANIC?
...
...
...
I THINK THIS CAN BE FIXED...
SPOILER ALERT— YANIC COULDN'T FIND A GOOD EXCUSE TO WEASEL OUT OF THIS ONE.

BOTH HE AND FOSTER GOT SUSPENDED.
I DON'T KNOW FOR HOW LONG.

NO ONE PETITIONED
TO BRING THEM BACK.

...THEY FREAKED OUT AND LAUNCHED A SCHOOL-WIDE "BULLYING AWARENESS AND PREVENTION" PROGRAM...

THIS IS DR. NUNEZ, A PSYCHOLOGIST. SHE'S HERE TO TALK TO YOU ABOUT—

...WITH, LIKE, CLASS SPEAKERS, "EMPATHY BUILDING" WORKSHOPS...

...AND REALLY WEIRD "TRUST-BUILDING" EXERCISES.
NOW PUT YOUR EGG ON THE SPOON AND GIVE IT TO YOUR PARTNER!
...
what.
hahaha

...I DUNNO IF IT'LL HELP...
...BUT I GUESS IT'S NICE OF THEM TO TRY.

...AND ONE GOOD THING DID COME OUT OF IT ALREADY.
H-HEY, JENSEN.

UH.
Y-YOU KNOW I DON'T **REALLY** MEAN ALL THAT STUFF I SAY TO YOU, RIGHT?
THAT I'M KIDDING?

...!

UH.
I GUESS?
...
I DON'T REALLY LIKE THOSE TYPES OF JOKES THOUGH.

C-COULD YOU STOP?
OH.
S-SURE.
WHATEVER.

SHE DIDN'T TALK TO ME
FOR A WEEK AFTER THAT...

...WHICH WAS
A BUMMER...
...BUT STILL
BETTER THAN
THE "JOKES."

...AND THEN, ON MONDAY—!
HEY, JENSEN,
I THINK I MISSED
YOUR BIRTHDAY
THIS YEAR.
HOPE YOU LIKE
CHOCOLATE!

...TL;DR—
WE GET ALONG
MUCH BETTER
NOW...

...AND THE DAILY SCHOOL
LEVEL GOT EASIER.

HI, JENSEN!
H-HEY.
...
HEY.
OH, HI, OLIVIA! HI, GUYS.
THE GAME MONSTERS ARE VERY CONFUSED.

...I WONDER NOW... IF THEY WERE EVEN MONSTERS AT ALL...
...OR JUST REGULAR PLAYERS, SAME AS EVERYONE ELSE...
DOES SHE EXPECT ALL THIS BY TOMORROW?
NO WAY...
...SIMPLY TRYING TO GET THROUGH MIDDLE SCHOOL.

...!
...FOSTER'S BACK?

...HE SEEMS DIFFERENT.

SHOVE

HEY, WEASEL, YOU'RE BACK.
WHERE'S YOUR BUDDY— HE LEFT YOU ALL ALONE?

U-UH...
HE'S STILL SUSPENDED, I THINK.
HA-HA, SERVES THAT RODENT RIGHT!

SEE YOU AT LUNCH, WASTE OF SPACE!
SHOVE
....!

. . .
SLAM

...I USED TO KINDA THINK THAT EVERYONE KNEW HOW TO GET THROUGH MIDDLE SCHOOL EXCEPT FOR ME...

...THAT THEY ALL HAD CHEAT CODES OR SOMETHING...

...AND KNEW SOME SECRET MOVES I DIDN'T.
JENSEN.

SOLID B+ ON YOUR LAST TEST. WELL DONE.
B+
....!
KEEP AT IT.

...NOW I THINK WE'RE ALL JUST TRYING TO FIGURE THIS OUT...
...LEVELING UP, ONE LITTLE VICTORY AT A TIME...

...CHANGING THINGS, ONE LITTLE BIT AT A TIME.
JENSEN, OVER HERE! NATHAN SAVED YOU A SPOT!

HA HA HA
hey, did you hear...
...I KEEP THINKING ABOUT THAT CULTURE STUFF AKILAH AND JENNY WERE GOING ON ABOUT.
I THINK...

...I'M STARTING TO SEE IT...
..."CULTURE OF ISOLATION"...
...PEOPLE GETTING LEFT OUT...

...AND HOW IT'S ALWAYS BEEN AROUND, IN SOME FORM...
GROUP PRESENTATIONS TODAY
MAJOR LEAGUE BASEBALL USED TO NOT LET YOU PLAY UNLESS YOU WERE WHITE AND MALE, UNTIL—

...AND HOW IT DOES GET CHANGED OVER TIME, JUST LIKE AKILAH SAID.
BUD FOWLER
ELIZABETH "LIZZIE" MURPHY
TONI STONE
PEOPLE CHANGING IT, WITH THEIR ACTIONS—

IN 19
FOWL
BECA
...
I WONDER IF THEY WERE EVER SCARED, TRYING TO CHANGE THINGS.

RRING
CHATTER
HA HA HA HA
BERRYBROOK SCHOOL
hey

...I DIDN'T END UP LIKING "MY BADLY DRAWN LIFE" AT ALL...

...BUT I **LOVE** INA CRUZ'S BOOKS.

"FIGHTER" IS MY FAVORITE ONE.

SHE TALKS A LOT ABOUT ALL THAT STUFF IN IT—

—ABOUT FIXING WHAT'S WRONG, CHANGING WHAT'S AROUND YOU, DOING THINGS YOU'RE AFRAID OF...

...ABOUT WHAT COURAGE IS.

"...BUT THAT'S WHAT COURAGE IS—NOT NEVER BEING AFRAID...

SURVEY QUESTION:

What culture would **YOU** want to build? What would be the norm there?

Which actions would help build this culture?

"BECAUSE WE ARE ALL STRONGER—

"—WHEN WE ALL LOOK OUT FOR ONE ANOTHER.

"WE JUST HAVE TO HAVE THE COURAGE TO DO SO."

THE END

NOW, THE END. (FOR REAL.)

WHEE!

CONGRATULATIONS!!!

(to me, for finishing making this book, and to you, for finishing reading it! ☺)

At this point you're probably seriously wondering 'what's the deal with these sunspots?! Why does Jensen care about them so much?!' Well, the back story here is that Jensen was doing research for a science class project once upon a time, about our solar system and especially the sun. To his SHOCK and HORROR, Jensen discovered the existence of...

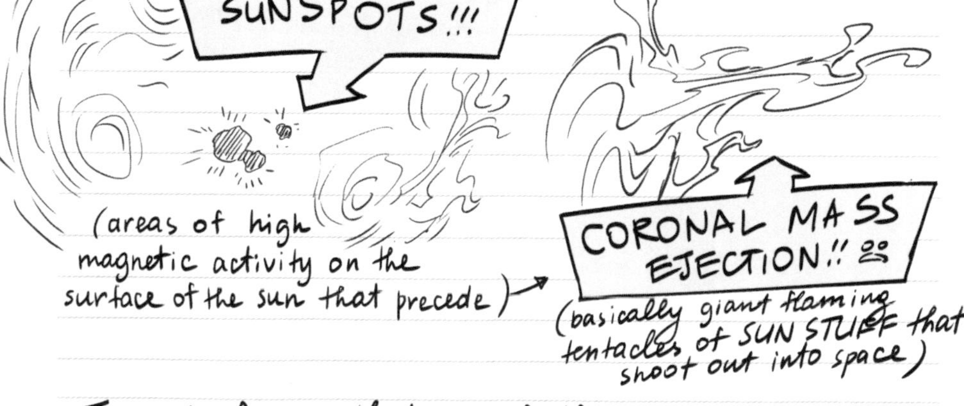

Jensen's fear is that one of these solar events could one day reach the Earth... And FRY IT TO A CRISP.

(IMPORTANT NOTE:
To my knowledge all that stuff is not a real danger to Earth, so hopefully Jensen is in for a pleasant surprise!)

Having said that, I can definitely relate to dealing with a deep-seated fear. (who doesn't have one?! They're lucky!) When I was about 11-12 years old, I was terrified of a large open maintenance well on the edge of my town.

It was an 8-10 foot drop to a strong foaming roar of dark rushing water.

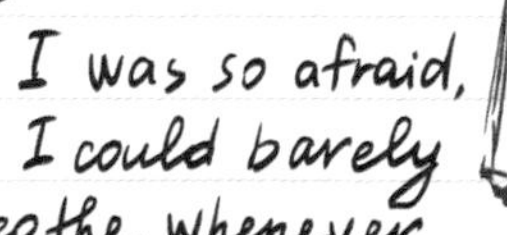

I was so afraid, I could barely breathe whenever I passed it — what if the water started rising? We lived near a dam and the water from the lake could totally flood my entire little town. I'd lie awake at night, wondering if it was going to happen NOW, while everyone slept. Was the dark cold water rising out of the well?!

(Spoiler—it wasn't. But I still had to slink out of my comfy bed to check and make sure.)

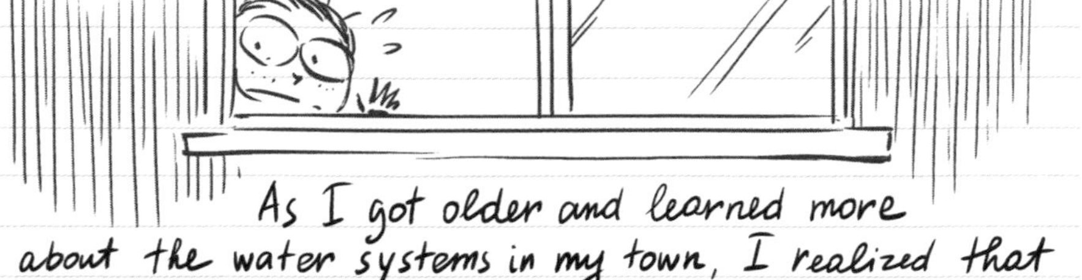

As I got older and learned more about the water systems in my town, I realized that what I was so afraid of couldn't really happen, phew! It's weird how learning about the thing you're afraid of can actually help you get over the fear.

...Well, that, and copious amounts of daydreaming and drawing. Which, like Jensen, I did a lot of, on a daily basis (and also mostly in school, hahaaaaa...)

...AND NOW I'M AN INTERNATIONALLY PUBLISHED AUTHOR OF 12+ BOOKS

so that all worked out okay.

Moral of this long-winded story: if you're afraid of sunspots and stupid creepy maintenance wells on edges of small towns, you may have a bright future as a writer and/or cartoonist?!

Stranger things have happened.

AND NOW!!! It's time for the...

SKETCH GALLERY!!

Before I start drawing a book, I always do tons of what is called 'concept sketching'.

It's basically a lot of loose, fast doodling, where the artist will try out some visuals of character ideas. And by loose doodling I mean <u>loose</u>. Barely legible. Downright horrible, really; so bad that I won't even include them here because I don't want you to go blind. YOU ARE WELCOME.

...But here are some rough sketches that are a step up from that and safe to look at:

Mrs. Crabbler was a lot of fun to design. She didn't end up in a lot of scenes in the book, so I was trying to capture her whole character/role in just a couple of self-explanatory drawings.

Jensen!!
I loved drawing Jensen SO. MUCH. I wish I could do a whole book of just his amazing daydream adventures in space, where he fights Mars zombies and discovers extraterrestrial civilizations.
Mrs. Crabbler's sister?!
no idea
Not all teacher designs made it into the book, but I still had fun sketching them. Better too many designs than not enough!!

Expressions are 99.999% of what makes a character, IMHO.
So I draw A LOT of them.
Felipe
colour streaks in hair?
Jenny and Akilah, the BFF series
reading comics, listening to music together
Very early newspaper crew sketches, just trying to get their personalities down, very loosely.
...And, last but not least, no sketch gallery is complete without Mr. Raccoon!

THANK YOU!

...to my husband, Patrick, who would bring me food and make sure I had everything I needed during the last relentless deadline dash; to Melissa, who REALLY burned that midnight oil to help color this book on top of everything else she had going on; to my editor, JuYoun, for too many things to count but especially for getting me more time; to my publisher, Kurt, for the faith in the face of no discernable pages; to the AMAZING Yen Press crew for making my stuff look professional and awesome; to Nancy, for the inside info on the nurse's office particulars; to my agent, Judy, for always looking out for me; and last but not least...

THANK YOU to all my family, friends, and fans who make the lonely hard work of making a graphic novel bearable and totally worth it.

AVAILABLE NOW!

AVAILABLE NOW!